What I Didn't See Before

A NOVEL

ALEXANDRA DAVIDSON

What I Didn't See Before

To Emma and Joe, for making life brighter when I didn't think it was possible. ♡

What I Didn't See Before

What I Didn't See Before

Chapter 1
May 30, 2019
Luca

The yelling from downstairs violently shakes the whole house. My dad's always been this strong, kind-hearted man I looked up to as a kid. I remember the thousands of times he took me to his work. All his co-workers picked me up, chased me around the office, and showered me with snacks. Then at the end of the day, he took me for ice cream as if I hadn't already had enough sugar. It's a shame that innocence has to come to an end at some point. I used to think Spongebob would stay my favorite show forever and that I wouldn't have to worry about making all these "grown-up" decisions. Sometimes I wonder what really made Dad the way he is now. He screams at my mom for everything and is constantly drowning himself in alcohol.

What I Didn't See Before

It all began three years ago when the small business he started earlier became a multi-million dollar company. Now he's the big gun, the driving force for the entire thing. So, in his world, our family is nothing but a distraction to him now.

Squeak. The door in my room cracks open a little. "Hey, seriously, knock before you-" I started to say but then saw my dog Cha Chi walking towards me with his tail down. "Oh hey buddy," I said. "Come here. Sorry, I thought you were Alaina." Ah, speak of the devil. Through the tiny slit of the door I see her walking my way. She pokes her head into my room.

"What do you want?" I ask harshly.

"Mom says you have to take me to Anna's house." Alaina's eyes fill with tears. I realize I can be a little snappy with her but isn't everybody to their younger siblings?

"Can't you see I'm busy?"

Alaina looks around the room and sees my T.V is on. "You're just watching that stupid sci-fi show."

Going out at 9:45 p.m. is the last thing I want to do right now. I just want to go to bed and hopefully wake up anywhere else but here.

"Fine. Get your shoes."

"Thanks, Luca!" Alaina's tears disappear in a decibel of a second and she runs down the hallway.

This is extremely typical of her. She's pretty sneaky for a fourteen-year-old. I know if Alaina goes over to her friend's house, she'll be good. She won't do the things I do when I go out.

"Luca! Come down here for a sec!" Dad yells from downstairs.

Okay, I take that back. Taking Alaina to her friends isn't the last thing I want to do. Going downstairs to face Dad is much worse. I guess getting out of the house wouldn't be so terrible right now. I have half a mind to jump out my window, but before I can do that, my Dad is on his way upstairs to my room. His drunken footsteps coming down the hall are too familiar. Suddenly, my door swings wide open. The force was so impactful that the doorknob dented the wall.

"When I tell you to come downstairs, you listen to me," Dad said nostrils flaring and a hard edge to his voice.

"Sorry Dad, I-"

"I don't wanna hear your excuses, boy. Next time just do what I say. You understand?"

"Yes," I say looking down at Cha Chi who's now hiding halfway under my bed.

"Good, glad we're on the same page. Now go take your sister to Anna's." I nod as he dizzily pivots around to leave my room.

"Alaina, you ready?" I yell across the house. Silence. "Alaina?" I shout again. Still nothing. My mind fills with the worst possible scenario. What if Dad hit her? What if she's hiding in the corner of her room after hearing the way he's acting right now? What if he did something terrible to her? He's not in the right state of mind and it's happened before.

I run all over the house to find her but then see through the window that my headlights are on. There's Alaina, sitting in my car eating a stack of Oreos. I laugh with relief and the fact that she has so many cookies in her lap. *Great, now I'm craving Oreos. So much for my diet.*

When we arrive at Anna's house she's waiting on the porch for Alaina, jumping up and down.

"Bye Luca, thanks for taking me!" Alaina says, Oreo crumbs still visible on the corners of her mouth.

She shuts the door without hesitation, then runs towards Anna and gives her a giant hug. Alaina and Anna have been friends for as long as I can remember. My mom met her Mom at the hospital when she was pregnant with Alaina and Anna's mom was pregnant with Anna. They bonded about their due dates being the same, the fact they were both having girls, that they lived in the same city, and way too many other things.

Buzz. I pick up my phone from the passenger seat, look at the road ahead of me and then quickly back down at my phone. *Shoot.* Dad called three times. How did I not hear that before? If I don't call him back right now I might as well not even come home. This happened before with my older brother, Devin. He was out with friends getting slushies and didn't check his phone. That was his first mistake- and his last. After the violent and intense beating he took from my Dad, he never left his phone on silent. Even though he's off at college six hours away, I'm pretty sure he still keeps his ringer on. It's just better that way. I dialed his number as quickly as possible, fumbling my fingers all over the keyboard. I must've typed the wrong number about twenty times.

"Shoot!" I yell at the top of my lungs, swerving as hard as possible back into my lane. The car across from me lays on their horn for the longest time and speeds away.

What I Didn't See Before

Whew, that was close. By this point my nerves are completely shot. I press the call button on my phone, anxiously waiting for Dad to pick up. No answer. I can't tell if I'm relieved or worried. I'd much rather have Dad scold me over the phone. At least that way he doesn't have access to beat me until my body is one huge bruise. I wouldn't have to hear Mom crying hysterically and yelling at Dad to stop. As I pulled into the driveway I was caught off guard because all the lights in the house were out. Mom stays in the living room every night to watch T.V or read until Dad is asleep. I'm crossing my fingers that she is okay, and praying Dad is asleep. I hate being the only kid in the house nowadays. Alaina's always with Anna, and Devin and Lila are off and college. Maybe I'd be out with friends more if I had any. Mazin is really the only person in my life I could put the label "friend" on. He used to have me over all the time so I could get away from Dad, but that doesn't happen much anymore after I started hanging out with a new group of guys.

  The living room is completely empty and pitch dark. I check the kitchen and dining area but it's also empty. *Oh. What was that?* A gentle voice I don't recognize is coming from my parent's bedroom. As quietly as I can, I

What I Didn't See Before

crack open the door. Mom is asleep in her bed with the T.V on and Dad is passed out on the floor with a toothbrush half hanging out of his mouth. I take the biggest deep breath and exhale a sigh of relief. When Dad wakes up tomorrow he's not going to remember what happened last night. Hopefully my long overdue beating can wait a while longer.

"Luca, wake up. Luca," my mom says impatiently. "Luca!"

Not the time, Mom. Not the time. I just don't want to get up and see the look she gives me every morning. It's a mix of self-loathing, disappointment, and fear. I know how hard all this must be for her. She has to deal with my problems and my Dad's. I think it's just the stress of final exams that spurred me to act like an idiot. I currently have all C's and a B so I guess I'm not drastically failing.

"Mom I'm not ready to get up," I say through my teeth.

"Honey, it's twelve twenty-three in the afternoon. You have things you need to get done. I need you to pick Alaina up, go run a few errands for me and start making flashcards for your finals. Okay?"

What I Didn't See Before

"Fine, sure, whatever." Even though I can't see my mom, I can imagine the look she is giving me. I toss myself sideways on my bed so I'm making eye contact with her. *Yup, there's the face.*

"Luca, I'm worried about you," she says with this voice that makes me feel guilty for a second. I don't know where the guilt is coming from though, but maybe it's because she gets treated like crap all the time. Maybe it's because two of the kids she's raising are huge disappointments to her. Maybe it's because she has almost absolutely no one in her life to confide in.

"Mom. Don't worry about me. I know right now this is all tough for you but I'm fine." I feel my heart rate elevate a bit because I'm lying to her. I'm not fine and I haven't been fine in a while. Now isn't the time to express all of this though, especially to my mom. She already has enough to worry about. And besides, I'm a man. Kinda.

"I know you don't want me to worry but it's not that simple. I feel like I can't help you. You never tell me what's going on. Just talk to me, I just want to help you when you're hurting." I can hear through her voice how much she wants this conversation with me but I really don't want to say anything to set her off.

"I'm fine, really." I'm lying again but it's a habit now. I've been lying to my family since I was a kid. It's just easier that way. It saves conversation and punishment.

Before she shuts my door she sighs loudly and cracks a fake smile. But once the door is shut my heart finally drops back down to its normal pace. I'm not much of a crier at all, so instead it's covered by annoyance and irritation. Devin always cried in front of Mom and still does. He's a grown man, but the most vulnerable guy you'll ever meet. Mom has hit me thousands of times with, "Devin, teach him to be more open like you." Or "Devin, you're so good at telling me what's going on. Why can't you do that Luca?" It drives me insane, but she's probably right.

Devin Grayson Matthews has been the one person in my life I look up to, but secretly hate. Well, it's actually not really a secret. It's fairly obvious to my whole family and all my friends. He's just really nice and it's weird. Anybody that's as nice as my brother I find really, really strange. Ever since we were kids, he was always the first to compliment my parents on their home-cooked meals, new haircuts, outfits, honestly, everything. My sister Lila and I actually had this ongoing competition to see if we could beat him to it. We lost every single time. As much as I wish I was, I'm not a people pleaser like he is. I can disappoint somebody and laugh about it. When I hurt somebody it doesn't hurt me back. The only thing that hurts me is seeing my mom like this and not being able to do anything about it. If Devin were here he would be fixing it within the minute. He'd probably take Mom shopping and buy her the expensive jewelry she's been wanting for three years now, or go on a morning run with her. I've never offered to spend time with her. It's just awkward though because we aren't close at all. She doesn't know a lot about me and I don't know much about her either. It might be for the best though. I don't know if she wants to know me. I don't even know if I know me.

    I don't belong at this party, especially because there are way too many people here I don't know. It would've been best if I said no to Garrett's invite and just stayed home and played Fortnite or something.

    "Luca! Come here, there's someone I want to introduce you to," Garrett said and gestured me over. I looked to my left and saw three people passed out on the floor with broken bottles around them.

"Hey make this quick dude, I really gotta get headed home soon," I said uneasily. The only thing this party has that I would bother staying for is the booze. I wasn't much of a drinker before, but it's become a habit ever since my mental health started declining.

"This is Cynthia. Cynthia, this is Luca. Go ahead and talk, I'm gonna go mingle. See ya guys!"

And just like that, he was gone. It's no surprise he left me alone with a pretty girl. Every single time we go to one of these things he's always trying to set me up.

"Garrett is something else," she said shyly. She smiles and tucks her short blonde hair behind her ear then reaches her hand out towards me. "Cynthia Morgan."

"Luca Matthews." I reach out and accept her hand into mine. My palms are extremely sweaty. She definitely noticed because she slyly wiped her hand on her shirt afterward.

"So, what's up?" she said walking away slowly but keeping eye contact so I would follow her.

"Uh, I don't know, not much."

"You look uncomfortable. How about I go get you a beer and you wait here."

What I Didn't See Before

"Thanks," I say with the fakest smile. I've been thinking of my mom too much to drink more than one beer tonight. I don't want to come home drunk when she already worries enough about my dad doing that too. Out of the corner of my eye I see Garrett spying on us. I whirled around to face him and gave him the famous 'I'm gonna kill you' look. He dismissively waved it off and gave me two thumbs up.

"Here you are," Cynthia says and hands me an ice-cold 4 loko. This is definitely the last thing I need to be drinking right now, especially with exams tomorrow. I shouldn't have even come here in the first place.

"Uh, thanks again."

"So, Garrett says a lot of good things about you. I mean, he practically gave me your life story. You've got some pretty incredible background to you."

"Not really." I don't have any cool stories, a cool background, or a cool family history.

"That's not what he told me. He said you escaped an armed robbery at gunpoint?"

I choke on my drink and spit it out, laughing hysterically. "What? No, no. No, that never happened."

"Okay, there you go," she said smiling and laughing with me.

"What?"

"I knew you'd have a great smile," she said, taking a sip of her drink and looking up at me.

We talked for about an hour and I didn't even realize how many drinks I gulped down in that time. I was starting to feel out of it, less self-aware, and my inhibitions lowered.

"So you play any sports?"

"Yeah, I'm the quarterback for the high school team."

"What high school?"

"Oh sorry, I figured you went to our school. Damon Ridge, where do you go?"

"I'm actually doing online right now through Damon Ridge. I still come into the school sometimes, like for tests and stuff. It's just easier for me to learn that way."

"Oh. Well that's cool too." At this point, she's just staring at me, deeply. I was staring back, returning the interest she was giving me.

"I know what you're thinking," she says with a little bit of hesitation to her voice.

"Huh?"

"I'm sorry if I gave you the wrong impression, but I kinda have a thing with someone right now. I was just being friendly. You seem like a great guy, but you're just not really my type."

Not my type. The three words that have made it impossible for me to have any sort of romantic fling in my whole lifetime. I'm seventeen years old and have never kissed a girl, let alone had a girlfriend, ever. *Am I really so repulsive? Is there something so disgustingly hideous about me that nobody will ever accept? It's got to be a physical flaw because this girl just met me and she's already saying those three words I hate.*

The alcohol takes control of me- the power I once had is now leaving my body and a new entity takes its place. I feel the red hot flesh rise to my face, my veins jolting with energy, and my stomach twisting into hundreds of knots.

"What's the matter with me? Why am I such an idiot?"

I started to let this entity take over because I can't control it now. It's bursting with anger and hatred, intensifying by the second. I feel like my whole body is ten feet tall and there is fire coming out of my skin that's willing to burn the whole house to ashes.

"Woah, calm down I just-"

"Don't you dare tell me to calm down!"

The entity is shouting now and apparently shouting loud because all eyes are on me. I glance over at Garrett who is completely taken aback that his little match-making game didn't work. Suddenly this entity runs at him. Garrett scrambles on his scrawny legs and tries to run towards the door but he's drunk too. Instead, he falls straight down. The entity grabs the front of his shirt and punches him square in the face. My eyes watch as Garrett grabs his bloody red nose, props himself upon his knees, and starts to feel around the floor for his glasses. I try to take control of myself as this thing inside me starts to go at him again, but then just as quickly as this all happened, I'm being pulled away by a crowd of sober drunks.

Chapter 2
May 30, 2019
Paige

"When you look at this picture, what do you see?" Dr. Woods asked.

"A blob."

"Paige. Think deeper."

"Okay." I inhale the hand sanitizer scented room and try again. "A blob with hands."

"Hm. I guess that's a little better," Dr. Woods says, rolling her eyes. She's a nice lady, really, I just know exactly where this conversation is leading and I'm not here for it.

"Okay." I hoped she'd just let me go.

"One more thing before you go, Paige. Have you tried forgiving your dad?"

There it is. "No."

"Think about it."

"Okay."

"Well, okay, have a good week. I'll see you tomorrow."

Dr. Woods led me out of her office and into the empty lobby. I used to think the aesthetic here was lonely; off-white walls with no picture frames, linoleum floors, and that strong scent of hand sanitizer that makes you believe your brain is on fire. But now, it's my home. I love the beauty of the minimalistic features, the long winding hallways, the view of the sunrise and sunset from the giant glass walls. Being here is what I'm used to, but I wouldn't change it for anything.

The long walk back from the psychiatric branch of the hospital to the hall where my room is located takes about seven minutes, just enough time to play a few rounds of mental tic tac toe. My favorite thing about mental tic tac toe is that you always win no matter what. It's a good distraction from thinking about all of the things I'm losing; my hair, my ability to think, my weight. Having cancer isn't the worst thing really, it's more so what the chemo does to you that makes things ten times worse.

"Paige, hey!" my best friend Joey shouted from his room. "Game night later in the teen room. See you there?"

"Yeah, sounds good." I started to walk away, but Joey is one of those guys who keeps pushing and pushing until you just have to finally accept that you're gonna lose so you just give in.

"Wait!" he shouted again. "Come back!"

"Why?" I said this with such annoyance that I immediately felt guilty.

"I can tell something is bothering you. Come on, sit."

He gestured me into his room and I pulled my IV stand in, accidentally knocking it against the walls. I felt a quick tug of the tube inside my arm when the stand got stretched too far away from me.

"Next time, I'm not coming in here until my IV is empty. Great, the machine is beeping." I pressed the nurse button, told her I was in Joey's room and she came rushing in.

"Paige, we've talked about this. Wait until your treatment is over before you go see your friends. Okay?"

Heather has been my nurse for the whole four years I've been living in this hospital. You'd think this would be one of those situations where you wouldn't be admitted to the hospital for four years straight, no going home, no public school, no nothing. For me though, I have one of the world's most compromised immune systems. In fact, according to my caretaker Dr. Mudrow, I have the second worst case he's ever dealt with before. Not to brag or anything, but it's cool having a title like that. Being experimented on though? I could live without it.

"Yeah, my bad. Well, Joey's bad actually," I said laughing.

"Oh, I see now. Well, it's all fixed. Please just wait until it's empty next time though. I'll be back to check your vitals in a little, just page me so I-"

"So you know where I'm at, yeah yeah. I got it."

She winked at me and walked off, closing the door behind her. I turned around to face Joey. "No infections I hope?"

"Of course not. You know I'd never invite you in if I had an infection."

"Do I?"

He laughed at me and then flipped his hair to the side. He's got this huge scar on his face that he usually covers up with his blonde floppy hair, but he lets me see it.

He says it's from when he tried beating this kid up in eighth grade but honestly, I think a kid beat him up and succeeded. I don't think he really 'tried' anything.

"So what's up? Lay it on me."

"Dr. Woods wants me to forgive my dad. She keeps asking me if I did."

"I see. Have you tried it at all?"

"No. Why would I after what he did?"

"Because that way you're one step closer to having peace of mind."

I felt the tears well up behind my eyes for a second but I forced them down, allowing the stone-cold me to come out. "I'll do it when I'm ready. I'm not ready yet."

"I know, I'm sorry."

Joey began to rub his neck, a nervous habit that for him triggers bad thoughts. He does this a lot, and has been working on it in therapy. I smacked his elbow with the back of my hand and wagged my finger in front of his face.

"Stop doing that. You gotta learn," I said.

"Aw, was I doing it again?"

We both laughed but were quickly interrupted by beeps from Fred, my IV machine. Yeah, I named him Fred. He's like this little fanboy who keeps me hydrated and

What I Didn't See Before

follows me around practically every single second of my life. We've become good friends, Fred and I. It was empty so I quickly flushed the IV out and capped it so I could leave Fred in the corner of the room without worrying that I'd pull the tube out of my arm.

  Joey's been here almost as long as me, about three and a half years. We've gotten to know each other pretty well since our rooms are right next door to each other. He's a year older than me, eighteen, and has leukemia just like me. It's really the only thing we truly have in common- that and the fact that we're both from Georgia- but that's what makes us great friends, we're polar opposites. I'm more of a southern raised kid, he's more of a city raised kid; I like the outdoors, he likes the indoors; I love horseback riding, he loves making fun of horseback riding. We have our differences, but we have never truly argued before. Besides, if we actually argued I know I'd lose because he's always right. Joey has this zesty personality. He never goes down without a fight. He once got an infection so bad that they had to put him on life support and somehow he still managed to fight it off.

  I remember that day so vividly. I wrecked everything in my room. I threw things, shattered glass

What I Didn't See Before

vases, ripped my IV out, pushed Fred into the door, and cried so hard that I could barely catch my breath. I felt like I was outside my body and this new thing stepped inside of me and took over. What's haunted me most about that day though was Heather's face when she came sprinting into my room. She grabbed my arm and started to sanitize the wound from my IV, worried that I'd caused an infection from ripping it out. She always puts my health first, before everything else she has going on in her life. It sometimes is hard for me even to imagine that she has a family she's taking care of outside of me.

"What're you thinking about?" Joey asked.

"I don't know. I'm thinking a lot."

"A lot of what?"

"Stuff."

"What kind of stuff?"

This is exactly what I'm talking about, he's very persistent. Always wants to know everything because he thinks he can fix it all, or maybe he just wants to try and fix it all for me. That's the kind of friend he is, someone who actually wants the best for you.

"I just think about last year all of the time. I know we're past it and you're okay now but I can't help but think of all of the what if's, you know?"

Joey scrunched his face, feeling guilty even though he'd done absolutely nothing. I could tell he was biting down on his tongue which is something he did a lot to stop from releasing any kind of negative emotions. It's another thing he was told not to do but he still does almost every single day.

"I'm still here. You gotta let this go, G. You have enough to be anxious about and I do not want anything relative to me to be something that worsens your mental health. I want to relieve it, okay?"

I nodded.

"Come here."

He grabbed my arm and wrapped his arm around me. I don't know many guys who love hugs, but Joey is an absolute teddy bear. He's great at having real discussions with me too, which is something I look for in people.

"You thinking what I'm thinking?" I asked.

He raised his eyebrow up a little and backed away from me, bobbing his head from side to side.

"No no no. I know what you're thinking but no."

"Come on, please!"

"No, Paige. I'm not doing this again. Do you remember what happened last time?"

He was walking away from me now but maintaining eye contact which is code for, 'I-know-you-are-going-to-make-me-do-it-anyway-but-maybe-if-I-act-all-scared-you'll-give-in'.

"Yes, I do remember. I also remember having a lot of fun though. Hey, you know, if you're gonna act like a baby about it I'll just go by myself."

"Good." He stood in the corner of his room underneath a Nike poster that said 'Just do it'.

"Okay, but before I go, look above you."

He spun around to face the poster and shook his head even more.

"Take your own advice, or don't. Whatever, hypocrite." I made my way out the door making sure not to look back because to him, that's closure. One thing he cannot stand is open-ended conversations which is exactly why my plan always works. I touched the doorknob and twisted it ever so slightly.

"Okay, fine! Fine, fine, fine, fine, fine." He snatched up his black leather wallet, frantically rushed around his room to turn off all of his lamps, and then grabbed his water bottle. "If this is really how you want to spend your day, okay. I can't argue with you. And maybe I did have a little fun last time but you know what would be even better? If we don't get caught. Or what would be even better than not getting caught? Not doing it at all. My nurse is gonna kill me, G."

I rolled my eyes and pulled his arm to follow me. "Don't be a wimp. Live a little!"

I'm a lover of practical jokes, and I know I'm helping him get to love them too. Last time we pranked the nurses by putting oil on the floor of the hallway and, well, you get the point. Nobody got hurt and it was all just harmless fun but boy did we get in trouble. So this time, I came up with an even better idea: it's foolproof. Nobody will get hurt.

"What's the plan?" Joey had this intense look on his face and was breathing so hard that I could practically smell the Doritos on his breath from a few feet away.

"Oh, ew, please don't breathe that heavily. It smells like nachos and it's making me want to vomit."

"This is making me want to vomit." Joey wiped his forehead like he was sweating or something, but he wasn't.

He and I don't really sweat that much since our bodies get depleted of water so fast.

"Alright, here's what we're going to do. Take this bag of marbles, they're plastic actually, because that way nobody gets hurt. You're welcome. We're going to the teen room," I replied, grinning mischievously.

"G, what if one of our friends falls for the prank and not one of our nurses? That could easily happen. I don't know if the teen room is the best idea."

"Trust me. I already told most of them not to open the cabinet. Kristina already spread the word, nobody's gonna open it. Plus, apparently, Donald is the nurse monitoring the room tonight. He's our perfect target! Come on, this will be fun."

"Donald is *my* nurse!"

"I know. It's fine. He'll laugh. Come on."

"So what, are we putting the marbles in the cabinet and then when he opens it they'll just spill all over?"

"Exactly. He's so jumpy and gullible, he'll be perfect! Now come on!" I tugged his arm and he trailed behind me until we were facing the door of the teen room. The teen room had always been my favorite hangout spot. Blacklights, purple walls, arcade games, leather couches, a fridge full of lots of snacks, and even a virtual reality station. It's where my friends and I hang out unless we are having bad days. Every so often we sneak in here at night and stay up talking for hours about the most random things. Last time this happened Kylee went on this long spiel about how her dad was slowly becoming obsessed with jelly- strawberry, not grape- she made that very clear.

"G," Joey was knocking on my arm with his knuckles. "Look." He pointed at a boy who looked about my age with brown hair, chiseled jaw, clear complexion and skinny but muscular. His face was bruised up and he looked like he probably had a broken nose. He was grabbing his stomach and making this terrible moaning sound. "He must've gotten into a fight or something. Looks pretty bad."

"Yeah."

The boy looked like he was in a lot of pain, like, a lot of pain. I don't know what happened exactly but if there is anybody who can find out stuff like this, it's me.

"Forget the prank."

"What?" Joey looked frazzled.

"I wanna find out what happened to him instead. We can play detectives or something, you know? That could be fun."

"But you already told everyone-"

"Yeah I know, I know, but we can just tell them that the prank is off. We can save it for another time or something."

"Are you sure? You were so into the idea like thirty seconds ago."

"Yeah, this will be fun. We can ask some of the others if they wanna be detectives too."

"You sound like a five-year-old right now, do you know that?"

"I know." I smirked and grabbed his arm. "Come on, let's go get Kristina."

Chapter 3
May 31, 2019
Luca

Everything around me was dancing. Fluorescent lights beamed down on my face, warming my cheeks a little bit. My eyes fluttered, they couldn't seem to make up their mind if they wanted to be open or stay shut. Two older ladies in scrubs stood beside me. One was injecting something into the IV in my arm while the other was drawing blood. I couldn't move even if I wanted to. Then I noticed my stomach felt and sounded like it was cooking something inside, all blistery and fiery and making churning and gurgling sounds.

"Luca?" A familiar face appeared in front of me. It was my mom.

"Mom, I'm so sorry. I'm really sorry, I don't know how-"

"Luca, it's okay, this isn't your fault. Who did this?"

"I don't remember who did or what happened. My stomach really hurts."

"We'll get you on some more pain medication soon to help," the woman with the square-framed glasses said. "I'm Dr. Huffman. Do you need anything right now? Thirsty?"

"Water would be good."

She smiled at me and walked away. I turned my face to see my Mom texting at the speed of light. Her fingers were moving up and down and from side to side, but her eyes kept rolling up to look at me. Finally, she stopped.

"I know you went to Garrett's party. Sean sent me a voicemail saying that you two got into a fight? He spent the night at the ER with a broken jaw and a concussion. I've never seen you act like this before, what's going on? Were you drinking? Either you were drinking or everyone around you was because you reek of alcohol. Was Garrett drinking? I told you that boy was a bad influence. I've always had such a bad feeling about him."

"I'm so, so sorry. I don't really remember anything," I stopped talking to grab my stomach again because it was all too much. Too many questions, too much to tell, too much pain.

"Do you not remember because you were drinking? Or do you not remember because you were knocked out?"

My mom has always had a way with me. She keeps asking and asking and pushing and pushing, but I've always been pretty good with just keeping it inside- or lying. But I was in too much pain this time to beat around the bush.

"I was drinking." I felt myself sinking deeper and deeper into disappointment. She was staring at me in silence with her hand over her mouth. I've seen her shoot me disappointed looks thousands of times, before but never one like this. It was enough to make a serial killer feel guilty.

"But you're such a good kid."

The words came out so softly, so full of melancholy. This was the most upset I'd ever seen my mom. I could tell she was trying her best to be calm but if I wasn't hurt right now, I'd be seeing anger spew out of every part of her.

Dr. Huffman walked back into the room with a small glass of water, no ice. I could see the condensation beads on the outside of it and the glass was foggy. It looked so cold, so refreshing, so much better than usual.

"Try not to drink too much, it could make things worse."

I've never appreciated water, but as I took the biggest gulp of my lifetime, I felt my lips curve upward a little bit, but she was right. It did hurt.

"So, Luca and Mom, we found the source of our problem here. It looks as if something triggered some very serious inflammation in your stomach that caused quite a bit of bleeding, so if you see blood in your stool, that's why. There is a severe tear in your esophageal blood vessel which can result in serious problems if we don't take immediate action. Surgery is our first step, then we'll have to start you on an NG tube so you can get your nutrition without complications. I'm afraid it looks like you'll be here in recovery for a while. Please be assured that we will make it as comfortable here as possible for you. We have a patient program here for teenagers in recovery so you can meet them later on. For right now, though, is there anything you can think of that may have caused this?"

"He was drinking, could alcohol cause it?" my mom asked, anxiety lacing her voice.

"Yes, an excessive amount of alcohol can cause gastritis and further complications as well. Alcohol tears the stomach lining down and in serious cases can result in something like this."

Dr. Huffman shifted her eyes towards me, and then back to Mom. She handed her a box of tissues. Mom thanked her and took one, burying her face in it.
"We need to start the surgery process now. You'll have to drink this." She handed me a metal cup full of liquid that looked like a vanilla milkshake. "It's Barium." *Okay, not a vanilla milkshake.* I tilted the cup and my head back and took a swig. It was *awful*. You could tell they tried to sweeten it or something but it tasted like I was drinking liquified chalk.

The nurse I saw earlier walked in and pulled Dr. Huffman aside. It was just my mom and I again, in silence, *again*. The cup of barium was still pretty full but I took my time drinking it because I was almost sure that it was going to fill up my throat. Once I was done, I sat the cup down on the table next to me when I saw this girl peeping through my window. She had brown hair, freckles, a slim face, couldn't tell much else. As soon as I saw her, she dropped down.

"Mom," I said, but when I looked over she was standing in the corner talking quietly to somebody on the phone. I shifted myself back over to look at the window of my room. The girl didn't pop up this time. Instead, there was a boy with dirty blonde hair looking in and once I saw him, he dropped too. I furrowed my eyebrows inwards and shook my head. I couldn't tell if it was all the medicine inside of me making me see things or if there were actually random teenagers stalking me. The girl popped back up again and saw I was staring at her so she waved at me and smiled. I felt the barium and the anesthesia processing inside of me and it became hard to move at all, so I just smiled. The boy popped up until his head was next to hers, and then another popped up, and then another. They all were smiling at me and just kind of staring for a minute until the girl with brown hair started to lip something to me. I couldn't tell what she was saying at all so I lipped "What?" back. She tried again, but was soon interrupted by a nurse who shooed them away from my window. I sort of hoped she was here for the recovery program even though she was probably just visiting a friend or family member.

She was pretty, and she seemed bold. A second later she popped her head back and waved goodbye.

May 31, 2019

I woke up to the sound of a machine beeping and something taped across my face. I slowly reached my limp hand up and felt a tube going up my nose. I also felt something tugging at my side, there was a tube there, too. I wanted to look down to see if it was going inside of my body, but I just assumed if I looked down that it would gross me out and I'd do something dumb, like try to tug it out. I felt so uncomfortable and all I wanted was to be back asleep.

"Good morning," Dr. Huffman said as she walked into the room and pulled out a rolling chair. "How are you feeling?"

"Um, fine I guess. Uncomfortable."

"I think that's fair," she said smiling. "But you'll get used to these tubes after a while. There was some fluid in your lungs which is why you have another tube down there. You'll need these for a while so you'll have to get used to them. A lot of my patients name them, it makes them feel like their tubes are their friends." I stared at her, expressionless. "But that's not for everyone."

"No, not a bad idea."

"Your Mom is out in the waiting room, I think you have some visitors here. Want me to send them in?"

I nodded. *Visitors?* I thought. *Not exactly sure who those visitors might be since I don't technically have any friends. I lost them, all of them. It's not like my dad would show up either, maybe my sister. That's really it.*

"Knock knock," my sister Alaina said and walked into the room. She was pushing a cart full of things: my belongings, clothes bins, decorations, curtains, a rug, even my stuffed animal I named James. He's a bear I got when I was in seventh grade, the day after my dad first hit me. Mom bought it to cheer me up and weirdly, it did.

"Oh, hi Alaina. You packed up my stuff?" I gave her a half hug because my whole body was still in so much pain.

"Yep! Everything you own. We're gonna make this room look great. Permission to paint?" Alaina glanced over at Dr. Huffman with her big puppy eyes like she does when she really wants something.

"Well, as long as we paint it back once Luca is discharged which looks like it won't be for a little while, so go ahead."

Dr. Huffman seemed a little agitated, but also impressed. Alaina is fourteen but she knows how to get what she wants, even if it means standing her ground to an adult. She doesn't do this very often to strangers, but it's nice that she cares.

"Great! Luca, I know you have no idea who these people are - to be honest, I'm not sure who they are either, but they just started talking to me in the hallway and well, now they're here, but they want to help decorate too." Alaina gestured towards the door and the three teenagers who were at my window earlier walked in. "This is Joey, Paige, and uh, Kristina, right? Kristina?"

"Yep! Nice to meet you, Luca," Paige replied.

She was smiling brightly, her teeth as white as pearls, no- snow. White as snow. Snow is whiter.

"Hi, yeah you too."

"So, I have no idea what happened but I heard you're gonna be here for a while, huh?"

"Yeah, apparently."

"Well on the bright side..." *If there is one*, I think to myself. "...those tubes will be just another part of your life like, say, clothes, in just a few weeks. Things get easier. They did for me, and they did for you guys, right?"

"Yeah, and this is a great place. We're all here for the recovery program so we've been here a long time. Everyone makes you feel at home here," Joey said.

"How long?" I asked.

"Well, I've been here four years. Joey's been here for three and a half, and Kristina one."

"That's a long time."

"It goes by fast," Kristina said smiling. "I know it's only been a year for me but it's been a good year. Hard, but good."

It seems like they've rehearsed this speech and are now presenting it to me. I know I should be flattered, but it's a bit weird how they're all smiling at me and talking about the hospital like they've been sucked into some sort of cult. Paige straight away caught my eye, and now that she's standing there smiling at me I'm a little embarrassed. I have bags under my eyes and I'm all bruised up from the fight, and to top it off, I can barely move at all from the pain. Even smiling is hard, so I'm just sort of staring back at her expressionless.

"Well, hey, let's get your room started. You just sit there and relax and we'll take over. Oh, do you like *The Beatles*?" Paige said.

"Oh, uh yeah, they're my favorite actually."

"This is gonna be fun. Joey, you mind grabbing the speaker from the teen room?"

"You got it." Joey gave Paige a little salute before dashing out of the room.

"Luca is obsessed with them. It's all he listens to," Alaina said, rolling her eyes.

"I don't blame him. I'm sort of obsessed myself. Favorite Beatle?" Paige asked.

"Mccartney. You?" I asked.

"Harrison. Favorite song?"

"Hard question. I like them all but my favorite has to be Across the Universe."

"That's my favorite too. It's so cosmic, but yet so earthly. You feel like you're floating when you listen to the lyrics."

"Yeah, it's always been my favorite."

What I Didn't See Before

Joey walked back into the room with the "speaker" which was actually an old-timey record player. It was a cherry wood color with a few names carved into it: Jim, Reagan, Iliana, and then I suddenly spotted Paige's name carved into it, bigger than all of the other names.

"Here we go, putting in the white album, a-ha. There!" Paige said and started to sing along to the lyrics of *Back in the U.S.S.R.* Then I realized I was too. I couldn't really move, but I felt my heart dancing. Paige was twirling around the room and using the paintbrush as a microphone. She came up to me every once and awhile, pointed it at me, and I'd sing the lyrics back and forth with her. *"Well the Ukraine girls really knock me out, they leave the west behind,"* and then I'd go, *"And Moscow girls make me sing and shout,"* and then in harmony we'd sing, *"That Georgia's always on my-my-my-my-my-my-my-my-my mind."*

Before I knew it, the whole room was finished. It was decked out, even better than the room I had at home. The walls were gray and light blue with accents of gold. I had a bookshelf next to me with four books in it. I've only read these four books in my entire life. They were "The Catcher and the Rye", "Things Fall Apart", "To Kill a

Mockingbird", and "Looking for Alaska". They're all very different, and I am perfectly aware of that. I've never been much of a reader until I started to write things myself. Then I became interested in reading other people's pieces so that's when I began reading.

"Do you like it?" Alaina was smiling at me, shifting back and forth from the balls of her feet to her heels.

"Yeah, it looks great. Thank you guys, you didn't have to do that." I made eye contact with everyone, but once my eyes hit Paige's, it was hard to look away.

"No thanks necessary," Paige said and smiled. Her smile was a little crooked, so kind, and so innocent.

Joey cleared his throat and grabbed Paige's shoulder. "Well, it's very late, we better get going. It was nice meeting you Luca. Once you're feeling better I'm sure we'll be hanging out all of the time. Our rooms are right down the hall if you need anything."

"Thanks, man," I gave him a head nod which he did back, and then he waved and they took off.

"Luca, what in the world?" Alaina was laughing, clutching her stomach and slowly crumpling to the floor.

"What? What's so funny?"

What I Didn't See Before

"This is a hospital, not a club. This is not where you pick girls up you dork."

"Excuse me?" I cocked my head at Alaina and then grabbed my neck letting out a quick *ouch,* before meeting her gaze.

"What?" Alaina was now laughing even harder. "You did that eye thing you always do when you want a girl. You know, the longing eye contact, the smolder face."

"The smolder face? God, Alaina, I do not make a smolder face at girls. That's really weird." She wasn't denying it though, she was on the floor with her knees to her chest laughing. I started laughing too because if there is anybody with contagious laughter, it's her. "Please tell me you're making this up. I didn't have a smoldering face, stop that."

"Oh yes, yes you did." Now she was completely serious and drying those happy tears from her cheeks.

Chapter 4
June 1, 2019
Paige

"Your turn, Paige." Kylee shifted her eyes in the direction of Dr. Donald.

We've always gotten a kick out of Donald. He takes his job very seriously. Don't get me wrong, but he's the biggest goof I've ever met. A lot of the doctors here are only focused on doing their job. They aren't emotionally involved with their patients. However, Donald has always had a soft spot for us. He loves us, and he knows we know that he loves us, and we know he knows that we love him.

I picked up a grape, sucked it in between my cheeks, and launched it. It hit Donald right on the top of his head and he quickly turned around. We ducked under the table.

What I Didn't See Before

"Bullseye," I said laughing.

"Nice one!" Kylee rewarded me with a high five, and then everyone did.

"Perfect aim as always," Joey said fist bumping me.

"What can I say. Never lost my touch."

I was a pitcher for a girls' softball team before I got sick. I was unstoppable. My team even gave me the nickname "The Force". My dad was the coach- I had a good relationship with him then- and he taught me everything I knew. But I was a natural. I was cut out for it. The first time I picked up a softball I was playing catch in the backyard with him. He caught it, looked at the ball, and looked up at me in astonishment. "Why haven't we played this before?" he said. "That's one amazing arm. Got that from your Dad, don't you ever forget that."

So my aim has always been good, but ever since cancer hit me I haven't been able to throw as strongly. My arms are thin and bony, and they're always fatigued. It's been a while since I've tried to gain arm strength back at the hospital gym.

"I want more soup. Anybody want more soup?" Kylee asked.

What I Didn't See Before

"I always want more soup. Don't worry about it. I'll go get you some." I grabbed my bowl and Kylee's and made my way toward the kitchen. Kylee has been very weak for a while now so anytime I can help out, I will. I'm weak myself, but compared to her, I am a lion. Kylee has leukemia like me, and she is severely anemic. We keep each other in check on the regular by eating food with tons of iron. So, in the kitchen, I snag her a stick of beef jerky and some dark chocolate as well.

It's a regular weekday here for us, not much happening, appointments around the clock, hanging out with the group for the whole day. Although I'm not sure how long Luca will be here, I'm hoping it's long enough that I can get to know him. Besides, Joey could use a guy to hang out with and talk guy stuff. He doesn't have any guys except for Eric, who comes around every once and a while but mainly hangs out with the other clique. Yes, I know it's surprising that a hospital would have cliques, but we do. None of us hate each other. We just don't exactly get along. Our group takes our health seriously, but not as serious as the other patients in the program. I don't want to be labeled as "cancer girl" or live like a cancer patient whose chances of surviving are slim. I'd much rather live as fiercely as I can, do whatever makes me happy, and believe my chances are as good as anyone else who is completely healthy.

Eric used to hang out around us before he needed an immediate stem cell transplant. We all stayed by his side throughout his time of healing, but he quit coming to teen groups, lunch in the cafeteria, breakfast facetimes, and just hangouts in general. He's spent a lot of his time alone in his room without anything but his video games which he doesn't even really play. I've made efforts to come visit him but he put a "Do Not Disturb" sign on his door. It's been hard not seeing him around lately. When we talk to Dr. Huffman about him she just says, "You all should be respecting his privacy. He would do the same for you."

Kylee took Eric's absence the hardest and despite what she says, she's still working through it. I know it was harder for her, and I started to believe there were some feelings between the two. They were always flirting with each other and laughing even when the other person's joke didn't make any sense at all. They would've been good for each other though. Eric is a good balance of being witty and stubborn, and Kylee is optimistic and assertive.

Eric was a privileged kid growing up. He always got his way as an only child with rich parents, but he was

What I Didn't See Before

learning from Kylee about how everything cannot just be given to you. To be honest, I think we all learn a lot from Kylee. She's protective of the people she loves and wants the best for everyone. If Joey ever shut me out the way Eric did, I likely wouldn't even give him a chance to explain himself. No matter how hard things get, Kylee has such an open mind about the "why" of things.

That's one reason I want to talk to Kylee about my dad. The only person who knows in our friend group is Joey, and he keeps pushing me to make amends but it's just so difficult. When your dad, your biggest supporter, the man you trust with your life, the one who taught you so many things like how to be tough, how to guard your heart, and how to forgive just up and leaves without any goodbyes, it's hard to trust again.

My therapist tells me very frequently to forgive him, to say out loud the words "I forgive you Dad" just so I'd be making some progress. How can I forgive someone who has never given me an opportunity to actually forgive them? He hasn't come back to make amends, he never told our family where he was going, and now my mom is drowning in medical bills trying to stay afloat without any help. So anytime Dr. Woods mentions forgiving my dad, I shut down. Everything becomes more painful and my mind starts racing.

Kylee is midway through her beef jerky when I notice she's staring at me. "You okay there?"

"Yeah," I spit out, even though I feel like I'm choking.

"I don't believe that at all, come on." Kylee grabbed my arm and pulled me to an empty table nearby away from our group of friends. "What's going on with you?"

"I don't wanna talk about it, okay?" I'm lying. I'm dying to tell Kylee what's going on. I can tell she's a little hurt after I snapped at her and I actually feel a little guilty. "I'm sorry. It's just hard to talk about."

"Hey, it's okay. We all have things we don't want to talk about, I just don't want you shutting down like, you know." She's talking about Eric, but I know mentioning his name would be too much.

"I couldn't do that. I promise," I stuck out my pinky to her and she wrapped hers around mine and gave it a little squeeze. "You'll be the first one to know when I'm ready to talk." She smiled at me and then something caught her eye around the corner, the girl from yesterday, Alaina.

"Paige!" Alaina shouted from across the cafeteria and proceeded to run towards Kylee and me.

"Alaina, hey, everything alright?" I could see a little bit of panic in her eyes.

"Yeah, hey everything is fine. Uh, it's just really kind of awkward for me to do such a thing. I'm not exactly the brave type you know, but Luca, my brother, wanted me to give you this." Alaina reached into her pocket, pulled out a wadded up piece of paper, and handed it to me. "I gotta run, they're gonna try and help Luca walk in a little while."

"Wait, Alaina, can I come with? I know getting back on your feet after not walking for a bit is pretty hard so I'd like to help if I can."

"Uh, sure. Just meet me in his room in like an hour. I'm gonna go and get him a smoothie up the street. He's been dying for a mango mania all day."

"They're letting him eat? That's great news!"

"Oh, uh, yeah they are I think. Anyways, gotta run." Alaina raised her arm as she turned and sprinted in the other direction.

"She's a little odd, yeah?" Kylee said laughing.

"They're letting him eat already? How is that even possible?"

"Paige, it's not. She's hiding something and I'm guessing it has to do with that thing in your hand."

I looked down at the note Alaina handed me and unfolded it.

Paige, meet me in the teen room tonight at 8:13 pm. Don't bring anybody but yourself.

-Luca

I stared at the note, frazzled. *Luca wants me to meet him? Alone?* I'm a professional at overthinking everything. Ever since I was in middle school and Bobby Fresca told me I looked like a boy when I started to lose my hair, I started to overthink every single thing. *Do I really look like a boy? Am I not pretty enough? When people see me out in public, are they scared of me?* I've worn a wig ever since that happened and make sure I never run low on makeup. If I'm starting to run out, I beg Heather to let me order it online to be shipped to the hospital.

So, why does Luca want to meet me? And if he sees who I really am, will he be scared too?

What I Didn't See Before

Chapter 5
Luca
June 1, 2019

I thought by now my dad would've at least sent me a text to check on how I was doing. To see if I'm alright. Even just as simple as a *"How ya doin kid"*, or a *"U good"* would work for me. He's not a lovey-dovey type of father, that's for sure. But for some reason, I expected something. I mean, my mom hasn't even left the hospital. She knows I'll be here for a while, yet she's been here in the parent area doing work off her computer. I'm not even sure when she last took a shower.

It's been nice not worrying about my dad coming home though. Here, I don't have to worry about hiding in the closet or standing right by the front door before he gets home just to protect my mom and sister. If I can protect them from taking a beating from my dad, there isn't anything in the world that would stop me from that. When I watched my mom get beat by him a year ago, I knew right then if I ever saw that again it would be my fault. I will not let him get near my mom when he's drunk. I will always be the one who waits for him by the front door and take the beating, and once he's done I'll clean up the blood and the shattered glass from the floor.

Before my brother left, my dad seemed to be cleaning up his act. He was always spending time with him. Taking him fishing, out to dinner, camping, and even came with him to buy his first car. In fact, he pitched in half. That's not at all how it went for me. By the time I needed to go buy my first car, I distinctly remember my dad looking at me and saying, "Why are you still standing here? Take your bike boy."

So maybe my life doesn't sound like the most wondrous, unimaginable fairytale, but I have an amazing sister who would go to the end of the world for me and an amazing mom who would do just the same, even though she clearly has a favorite child. I wonder if Devin knows what's going on. If he knows, I wonder if he would even care enough to text me.

Suddenly, Alaina comes bursting through my door with a smoothie. She's dripping in sweat and gasping for air.

"Alaina, what on earth?"

"I'm fine, I'm fine. Wow the A.C. feels nice," she said slumping into the chair and closing her eyes.

"Did you walk to the smoothie shop?"

"Almost. I ran."

"Alaina, it's like 95 degrees outside!"

"Yeah yeah, you think I don't know that? Sorry, you can't have this. It's mango mania. Your favorite," she said, accentuating the fact that it is my all-time favorite drink. She unwrapped the straw, stuck it in the smoothie and took a huge gulp.

"Are you trying to torture me or something?"

"No, I actually came with something else for you." Alaina walked closer and handed me a wadded up piece of paper.

I looked up at her, confused, and she threw her hands up at me.

"What? What are you waiting for? Just open it!"

I unfolded the piece of paper and began to read.

"What is this?" I asked looking up at her.

What I Didn't See Before

"What? I was told to give it to you so I did." She was staring at me very intensely like she was offended that I even asked her that question.

"Paige told you to give this to me?"

"Yeah, why? What does it say?" She walked up beside me and bent forward squinting her eyes and then read out loud, *Luca, meet me in the teen room tonight at 8:13 pm. Don't bring anyone but yourself...* "Huh. Weird."

"Yeah. Weird," I say sarcastically, knowing Alaina probably did this herself. She's always butting into my business.

"Well, I gotta get going. I would love to stay and catch up with my wonderful brother, but I have some work to do." She gives me a quick peck on the cheek and is halfway out the door before she turns around to say one more thing. "Oh, and Luca? Don't go trying to pick Paige up. Remember, this is a hospital."

I roll my eyes and check the time. It's 6:25 pm. Exactly an hour and forty-three minutes until I have to meet Paige in the teen room. Thing is, I have absolutely nobody here to help me get ready. The only way I could even shift positions on my bed is if someone came in and helped me.

So, how on earth does Alaina expect me to get dressed or let alone brush my hair?

I grab my phone from the table next to my bed and dial Alaina's number. No response. I call again. No response. *Okay,* I mutter to myself. *Looks like I'm doing this on my own.*

With all my strength, I pull myself to the side of the bed and put my feet on the ground. My whole entire body is completely numb from all the medication. I can't even tell if I am touching the floor. As soon as I tried to stand up, the room filled with stars. Everything got darker and darker, and darker, and suddenly I hit the floor.

My IV machine unhooked and began to beep. I tried to pick myself back up but I physically couldn't help myself. Suddenly, a nurse came rushing into the room in full-blown panic. She called for someone else down the hall and the two of them rushed to my side to pick me up.

"Oh my goodness, honey are you alright?" The young blonde nurse asked.

"I'm fine, sorry," I said empathetically.

"What are you doing? Why are you trying to get up? You're supposed to stay in bed. If you need to get up in the future please just phone us in. There's a button on the remote control attached to your bed. We can't have you getting hurt under our watch."

They were able to get me back up onto the bed, but I still felt like I was floating. I felt nothing. Feeling this way was alarming. *Is this what it's going to be like for me forever? Feeling absolutely nothing? Numb? Unable to feel pain? Unable to feel at all?*

"Luca?" The young nurse waved her hand in front of my face, snapping me out of my trance.

"Sorry, um I was trying to put on a change of clothes."

"Good lord kid. Okay. Just ask for help, okay? That's what we are here for." The other older nurse who wasn't talking at all nodded at me and smiled, and then walked back into the hallway. "What clothes do you want? Tired of the scrubs I'm assuming?"

"Yeah, I just wanted to put on something a little dressier."

"Dressier? How come? Got a hot date or something?" She laughed and I laughed too but little did she know that that's exactly what I had. A hot date. Sort of.

"Just wanted to make myself feel a little better, you know? Less like I'm at a hospital, more like I'm at home."

What I Didn't See Before

"I getcha'. Heather by the way. I'll be your nurse. But I have rules, okay? If you need help, ask. Don't try and pull these stunts on me, mister. Just phone me in. I'll be more than happy to help, capeesh?"

"Capeesh," I said smiling. "So do I call you Heather or Nurse Heather?"

She walked over to my "closet" which is just a hospital cabinet filled with my clothes from home. She started to rummage through my t-shirts and shorts, looking for something for me to wear. "Just call me Heather. That's what I tell all my patients. Everyone used to call me Nurse Heather but as soon as this program started here with all of the teens, I told them to refer to me as Heather. Made me feel more like a friend who was there for them and less like someone who gets paid to do this."

"Yeah, that makes sense. So you like what you do?"

"Like it? I love what I do. I was told I couldn't have any kids of my own a couple of years ago, so the kids here are like my own. I would do anything for every single one of them no matter how much anxiety they give me at times. Like you just now. I haven't even officially met you yet and I'm already feeling the momma bear come out."

"I'm really sorry."

What I Didn't See Before

"Don't be. You have a lot of Beatles shirts. Reminds me of another one of my kids, she has so many of them."

"Paige?" I ask.

She turns to face me and tilts her head. "Yeah, you know her or something?"

"Yeah, she actually helped paint and decorate this room with some other kids. We listened to Beatles music the whole time. They're my favorite."

"So you've already met some of the kids then, good! Paige is always helping other people. Must've been her idea to do all of this for you. Super headstrong. Man, can that girl assert herself."

"You think it was her idea?"

"Oh, definitely. I've known her for a long time. This outfit okay?" She's holding up one of my favorite Beatles shirts and a pair of khaki shorts.

"Yeah, yeah that's good."

"Okay well, I'm gonna face this direction. Sit down, whatever you do, do not stand up. We gotta start working on getting back that strength early. Try your best but if you need help I'm right here."

As I tried to get changed, I grazed my hand over my stomach. I couldn't feel anything. I touched my feet-couldn't feel anything. I touched my throat- couldn't feel anything. It took me nearly fifteen minutes just to put this shirt on.

"Heather? Is it normal to like, not feel anything?" I asked while pinching my leg.

"You're on Versed right now. It's a medication that numbs you, nothing to worry about."

"Am I gonna be on that for a long time?"

"Just during surgeries, any other time you're feeling pain we will just use some Lidocaine. Are you feeling okay? Any confusion?"

"Just a little dazed, that's all."

"Well, you better get to bed early tonight. You'll feel better in the morning, the medicine will be worn off by then. As long as you stay in this bed, there should be no complications." *Well, I won't be staying in bed. I'm not gonna let Paige down.*

I zipped up my fly and smiled. "Alright, all dressed." Heather turned around and saw me fully clothed. She put her hands over her mouth and then started cheering for me.

"You did that so quickly! It usually takes people days to have enough strength to do that. Two days, Luca. Two days. You, my friend, are a rockstar."

I was able to comb my hair, gel it back, and give it a little *swoosh* in the front. Sure, it may have taken me a half an hour due to the many breaks I needed to take because my arm would get tired, but I'm proud of myself. It's weird how after something like this happens you celebrate the teensy tiny victories.

All of the sudden a knock sounded at my door. I checked the clock, *7:58 pm*. I scoffed. I don't have a lot of time to stay and chat, I have 15 minutes before I need to meet Paige.

"Come in," I said with a little bit of annoyance.

A girl with auburn hair and freckles opened the door. She was holding a flower bouquet and dragging her IV stand behind her. She looked very frail, like if you poked her she would crumble to the ground. Her bones were very visible, especially in her face. The hair was clearly fake, it looked like a wig, but an expensive one. She also had a tube in her nose just like me, a rash that was clearly visible on her chest, and some bruises on her legs. It made me sad to even look at this girl, who was probably around my age. It looks like all the life she once had was sucked out of her, leaving her fragile and sickly.

"Hi, I'm Kylee. You're Luca, right?" she said smiling.

"Yeah, that's me." I returned the smile and she automatically warmed up.

"Thank goodness, I was afraid to walk into the wrong room. These flowers are for you to give to Paige tonight. I'm here to get you there safely. Here, they're lilies," she said, handing them to me. "Paige's favorite."

"How do you know about us meeting up?" I asked, curiosity getting the best of me.

"Paige told me. You're welcome for the flowers by the way."

"Oh, sorry, yeah thanks. Did she really want to meet up with me or did my sister do all of this?"

"Uh, no. Paige's idea."

"Why?"

"This is just her thing, you know? A new person comes into the hospital in our hallway and she wants to get to know them. She's always making friends. She just wants to make you feel welcome here."

What I Didn't See Before

"Oh, okay." So not exactly what I was thinking, but maybe that's a good thing. I probably shouldn't be hitting on a girl in a hospital, especially when I look like this. All beaten up, a black eye, a broken nose, and unable to feel anything.

"I'm also here too though if you need to talk to anybody. I'm sure any of the other kids here would be too. Paige is just sort of a natural leader when it comes to new people coming in. But she's a rule-breaker, so we need to get you there without any of the nurses seeing since you're not technically allowed out of your bed yet. Before I try to help you into the wheelchair, do you have any pain? Anything that would make it a bad idea to leave your bed right now?"

I swallowed back mentioning the fact that I couldn't feel anything right now. I wasn't going to miss an opportunity to get out of this room and talk to somebody else. "Nope, I'm good."

"You don't say much. A man of few words I'm assuming?"

I shrugged. "I guess so."

"Well, Paige is the complete opposite so just prepare yourself. She's gonna want you to talk more than you're talking right now." She looked at me with her hands on her hips, her bony arms sticking out on the sides. "Let's get you in the chair."

I swung my legs over the side of the bed, grabbed my phone, and slid it into my pocket. My feet hit the ground and my knees gave out.

"Woah," Kylee rushed to my side and helped me up into my wheelchair. "Have you started working on getting your strength back yet?"

"No," I said and started laughing. "But I did get dressed on my own."

"Hey, that's better than nothing! Always start with baby steps, and never ever try to get by all by yourself."

The walk down to the teen room- or should I say ride down to the teen room- was nice. It was good to get out of my bed and roll around the hospital. Kylee took me by Joey's room, who by the way was very confused where I was going with a flower bouquet, and she took me by Kristina's room, who was reading the biggest book I've ever seen. The people I've met here are like the most genuine people I've met in my life. All of my friends at school are the complete opposite and are mostly concerned with girls, parties, popularity, and sports. Sure I like girls,

What I Didn't See Before

sure I like sports, and maybe a party once and awhile, but popularity? Nope. I've learned it's the worst trap to fall into. Gets you in trouble and there is no benefit to come from it. I'm always at parties, never spending time with family, and I have no real friendships in my life. Yet for some reason, these people here want to get to know a loner like me.

What I Didn't See Before

Chapter 6
Paige
June 1, 2019

The past couple of hours have been me trying to clean up the teen room, get ready, avoid my friends, and read the new book my brother bought me. I know my mom picked it out because he is way too young, but it's nice to know he had the idea to get me something.

Avoiding my friends has been a bit odd. I'm so used to being with them every waking moment while I'm here. Joey has texted me twice asking if I wanted to get some Jello in the cafeteria, and both times he texted I ignored him. I could answer if I wanted to, but I'm terrible at lying. He always knows when something is off, even if I think I did a good job hiding it.

What I Didn't See Before

I've gone to the teen room twice now with Kylee just to make sure everything was in place. I'm assuming Luca isn't as much of a neat freak as I am, so I just want to make sure I'm not tidying up as he and I are trying to have a conversation. I definitely don't want him thinking I'm not into his invite.

I'm usually always the one to initiate a friendship with a new person, especially here at the program. When I first got here, the groups were so tight-knit there was absolutely no wiggle room for me. I spent a long time trying to find my place, but I eventually just gave up and mostly just spent time alone or with Heather. Not a lot of people take interest in a girl who would rather spend time listening to rock music than making friends.

A lot of that changed for me when I met Joey. He got here shortly after me, and we clicked right off the bat. Then all of these new people started piling in and a lot of the old ones were able to go back home. I started to hate the feeling of being isolated after I met him. I appreciated having friendships so much more once I got to know what a true friendship felt like. Ever since then, he and I have not left each other's side.

What I Didn't See Before

I flipped around to check the clock on the wall. I had 15 minutes to get there. I'm not too sure why he wanted to meet me or what makes him think he can leave his hospital room, but I'm extremely curious to find out. The last thing I want for him is to pull any stunts. Trust me, I've seen that happen all too often. My brother, Brayden, used to jump off the loft of our barn into piles of hay at the bottom. Maybe it seemed fun at the time for a six-year-old, but he ended up with a broken arm and a fractured rib. I've never seen him more lifeless than when I found him lying there. He usually has a pretty good pain tolerance, but this time he was struggling. He could barely say anything, just lying on the floor staring at the ceiling and holding his arm.

I looked in the mirror one last time, shut off the LED lights I installed to make my room more colorful, and took a deep belly breath. This is something we learn a lot about here. When you're anxious, nervous, or just simply not feeling good, a deep diaphragmatic breath can turn that all around. I have a very precise schedule to make sure I get in three ten minute sessions of deep breathing a day. I usually do it right after meals because it helps my digestive system function better. I swear by it. People might call me crazy, but it's a life-changer.

What I Didn't See Before

On my way down to the teen room I make sure to avoid all my friends' rooms so they don't catch me. Dodging Joey's texts is harder than I thought it would be. Pretty sure out of all the years I've known him I've never ignored a single text. The only time I ignore him is when he reminds me to talk to my dad. It's the only thing that comes out of that boy's mouth that I never entertain. He'll say, "Talk to your dad, it might be good for you." Or, "Paige, you owe him this." I don't owe him anything. If he chose not to be a part of my life, I choose not to be a part of his. Honestly, his loss. I'm a phenomenal daughter.

I don't know a lot about Luca, I don't even know what happened to him or why he's here. I've always been sort of a caretaker though, it's just a part of my nature. So when I saw him come to the hospital and learned he'd be staying here for the program, I knew I had to do something. Something to make him feel welcome and cared for. All I want to do is make sure he continues to feel that way.

When I talked to Alaina before we came in to help decorate Luca's room, she told me a little bit about him. A little bit about how he's always putting others' needs before his own and it leads him to make bad decisions for himself. A little bit about how his self-esteem isn't the best and he

What I Didn't See Before

tries to raise it in the wrong ways. She said all Luca wants is for her to have a good life. She made it very clear that he is very important to her and would do anything for him. She honestly reminded me a little bit of myself. A little stubborn, very honest, headstrong, outgoing, fun, and caring. I have a lot of those characteristics, especially being stubborn. If I want something, I'll find a way to get it.

It's 8:15 now and I'm waiting in the teen room for him. There is a small pit in my stomach- like that feeling when you go down a steep roller coaster- and my cheeks are starting to turn a little bit red. My hands suddenly started to tremble, more and more until the room was filled with stars. I knew exactly what was happening, it's all too familiar. *But now? Why now?* I heard a click at the door so I spun around- a little too fast.

"Paige?" Luca's voice echoed over and over again. My ears were ringing, my chest tightened, and my lungs were dying just to get a little bit of oxygen. Seconds later, my knees dropped to the ground and I saw nothing.

"103," Heather said nervously.

"Oh no, that bad? Is it my fault?" Luca cried.

"No hon', it's okay. Things like this happen. She's gonna have to be quarantined for a while. You did the right thing by calling me in."

"I'm so sorry, this is my fault. My sister wrote the note and I guess I went along with it."

My ears perked up at this. "Your sister wrote the note?" I squeaked out.

"Oh, you're up! Thank goodness, how are you feeling?" Heather said and rushed to Paige's side.

"Eh, could be better, could be worse."

"Let me go grab you some water, I'll be right back." Heather winked at me and closed the door behind her.

I turned to face Luca who was making eye contact with me, but I could see the regret in his eyes. "I'm sorry, Paige."

"It's not your fault. Don't be sorry, please. I do things like this all the time. I came because I thought you wrote the note for me."

"Well, my sister is a bit of a punk."

Luca smiled, and I breathed out a laugh.

"She reminds me of myself a little bit. I would've done something like that too, but unfortunately I'm the older sibling so I have to set a good example."

"Brother or sister?"

"Brother," I said, sitting up a little bit. "He's eleven."

"Bummer. We totally could've got back at my sister and set your brother up with her."

"That would be torture for Alaina."

"I'd be okay with that."

I rose my eyebrows, opened my mouth in shock and said sarcastically, "I guess I'll just have to tell Alaina you said that."

Luca laughed and shook his head. "What's your brother's name?"

"Brayden. Haven't seen him in almost two months."

"Why not?"

"Well, I haven't seen my mom in two months either. They come and visit once and a while to check on me but she's always so busy with work that she rarely has time to come up and see me."

"You miss them?"

"Yeah. I do. I've gotten so used to only seeing them once in a while but I do miss them."

"What about your dad? Do you see him?

What I Didn't See Before

    I took a huge gulp and thought of how to avoid this question without sounding rude. I don't want to talk about my dad and I certainly don't want to with someone I just met. He wouldn't understand what it's like having a dad who's not there. A dad who left and never said why. A dad who doesn't want anything to do with his kids. A dad who isn't *present*.

    "Uh, what? Sorry, I zoned out."

    "I said what about your-"

    "Back with your water!" Heather walked back through the door and I sighed heavily in relief. *Thank God.*

    "Thanks," I said, grabbing the water from her hand. I made sure to give her my wide-eyed signal which means *"I need to talk to you alone."* She picked up the hint right away and gave me a tiny head nod.

    "Okay, well we should probably let her rest and leave her be. I need to give Paige her treatment, Luca, but you're welcome to stop by tomorrow. That is if you ask *me* to come get you. Don't try to do everything yourself, understood?"

    "Understood, ma'am. See ya, Paige".

    "Bye Luca, and thank you."

"Anytime." Heather then pushed Luca back to his room.

Chapter 7
Luca
June 1, 2019

"That's not what I meant," I said, rubbing my forehead.

"Why not?" Alaina persisted.

"What is with you? She's really sick, Alaina. Let her rest."

Before I could even finish my sentence, she slammed the door and left my room. Alaina has always been the type to want to keep going after the matter-of-fact. Paige is sick with a virus she caught somewhere in this hospital, and who knows if I'm carrying it around too. I'd rather not be responsible for getting a patient here sick, especially one I think might have cancer. I haven't directly asked her yet, but I'm almost certain that's what it is. Her hair is definitely a wig- there is no way that's her actual hair. There's no frizz, no grease, and it looks so silky. I've always been a good-hair kind of guy. When I was really young, I let my hair grow down to my shoulders. That was an interesting time in my life. I barely had any friends, in fact, I was actually in the nerdy group at my school. My life revolved around my saxophone- yeah that's right. I was a band nerd.

  Since then a lot has changed. I cut my hair, got started on Accutane, and tried out for basketball. I made the team and that was when life took a drastic turn- this was all right around the time my dad got promoted. He never showed up to my games, started coming home drunk, and that's when he started beating me. So, by the time freshman year rolled around, I started making bad decisions. The basketball team was invited to every party you could think of, so I went. I got hooked on the scene of the party- the girls, the music, the alcohol, the drugs- all of it. However, I never got into any heavy drugs or anything like that, just vaping was it for me. It's been a while since I've actually done that though and I could live without it. Ever since the accident, I'm not really sure what to make of my decisions.

What I Didn't See Before

All I know is that whatever I did at that party cannot be erased and I need to figure out who I really am.

Paige seems like the type of girl who doesn't judge easily. In all honesty, I need more people like that in my life. I get too close to the ones who judge and persuade you into doing all sorts of things you don't want to do.

I roll over to the side of my bed and see my phone sitting on the table. Since I've been here, I've not been on it other than to check the time or to see if my dad texted. I've been oddly preoccupied with "hospital shenanigans". I snatch the phone from the table and slowly roll onto my back. I have even fewer notifications than I thought. Not a lot of people texted me, just a couple from my mom asking how I'm feeling, one from my friend Matt, and one that stuck out like a sore thumb- one from my brother Devin.

Hey kid. Heard what happened. Call me when you are feeling up to it. Be safe in that hospital. Love you little bro.

There's a part of me that really wants to call and talk to Devin. He actually might have some good advice to give right now, and I could use it. I wonder if he'd be awake though, it's 1:23 am, and he has a very particular sleep schedule. I get too distracted by my own thoughts and don't even attempt to maintain one. Comedy television keeps me up all night and when I finally get tired, it's daytime again.

I press dial anyways and wait to hear voicemail since it's so late, but instead, he picks up.

"Hey Luca," Devin said tiredly.

"Hey, were you sleeping?"

"No, just resting my eyes." I could feel him smirk through the phone. "I left my phone on my dresser with the volume on full blast so I wouldn't miss your call."

"Thanks. How's law school going?" I ask, trying to avoid my own problems.

"It's good, busy, but good. How's the crippled life going?"

"Very nice."

"Oh yeah?"

"Yeah. I love not being able to feel anything."

"Geez, man. Completely numb?"

"Basically," I said, sighing loudly. "I mean, if someone threw a brick at me right now I'd probably feel nothing."

"Is that so?"

"Pretty much."

"Well, you just gave me the biggest excuse to leave campus for the weekend."

"Wow. Me being in the hospital isn't a big enough excuse? You wanna throw bricks at me on top of that?" I laugh, and so did he. We've always had this back and forth banter between us. When it's time to be serious though, all of the fun disappears from him. Then it's just me acting like an idiot.

"You know how you make the best of your time there?"

"How?"

"Do some personal reflection. Do you like how you've been acting lately? Do you like your friends? *Do you like yourself?*"

And, there you go. Typical Devin, always has to lay something like that down on me.

"Uh, I don't know. Have you written a philosophical book yet?" I joked.

"I'm serious, Luca. Do you see where you're at because of your decisions? Alcoholic Gastritis. That's serious bro. Do you know what that can lead to?"

What I Didn't See Before

"Okay, okay, yeah I know," I say even though I don't know what it can lead to, and I don't want to know. "I messed up. Okay? I'm human."

"So am I."

"Dude, really? What's that supposed to mean?"

"I mean, I did stuff like that back in the day. Sophomore year mainly. I'm lucky I found the right people at the right time otherwise I don't know where I'd be."

"You? You used to go to parties and get drunk? Try and hook up with girls?"

"Women," he corrected me.

"Right, sorry, women."

"Yeah, I did. I wasn't very successful with the ladies though."

"Ha… me neither." I laughed.

"I'm serious. One woman pretended she was deaf. Started doing some made-up hand gestures to me, but little did she know I took sign language and she wasn't saying crap."

"Ha! Oh no. What did she say?"

"What do you mean?"

"You didn't tell her you knew she was lying?"

What I Didn't See Before

"Of course not! Always let the woman be right even if it kills you, because most of the time, she is right."

"Well, that one wasn't."

"No, no, she was right. I was a teenage boy, she was a smart beautiful lady. Best she didn't get involved with me."

Huh. He's making some sense. I hadn't talked to Devin like this in forever.

After Devin and I talked I grabbed a notebook from my bookshelf (which was just within reach). It was a manly journal with a black leather cover, no title, no cheesy motivational quotes- just simple. I decided to make a journal entry. I don't know the rhyme or reason that prompted me to do this, but I had an overwhelming motivation to write about myself. I felt the need to address the parts of me that need work.

Devin is devoted to God and gave his life to Jesus about two years ago. He's been working as a youth pastor at a Non-Denominational Christian Church. Personally, I have no idea who Jesus is. Growing up we went to a Catholic Church but I didn't understand what was being taught. I felt I was being punished when I went. The

Sunday school teacher used to tell me I was "unfixable", and "a permanently troubled kid". This worried my mom and dad at the time and they started to believe I was too far gone to be saved. Ever since then, they started leaving me at home. I was alright with it, a babysitter named Oliva used to come over and watch me, and I had the hugest crush on her. In some ways, Paige reminds me of Olivia. Olivia used to tell me I was never too far gone and that I was just young and reckless. She said she was once like that too.

But now I am older. Everything I did eventually brought me to this point in my life and I feel there is a reason for it. Although I'm not quite sure what that reason is, I think I have the right people around me to help me figure it out.

Last night Kylee gave me her number so I could text her about how the "date" with Paige went. She said she would text me first but she hadn't yet, so I decided to text her. I sent her a brief message about how Paige had a flare-up because she got a virus and that she was in quarantine now until it went away. Kylee was super helpful to me last night and even took me by the teen room before Paige got there so she could show me around. When we got there, everything was in place. The pillows were perfectly arranged, the blankets folded nicely and thrown over the backs of the couches and the games were color-coded on the bookshelf. Kylee mentioned that Paige dragged her there beforehand so they could make it look nice. When I asked Kylee why, she mentioned that Paige was very peculiar about how things looked, no matter who was going to see it.

After writing Kylee, I spent 30 minutes writing my very first journal entry. It felt weird to grip the pen in my hand and not get a cramp after five minutes. The numbness was taking over my body at this point, and my eyes were growing weary. The silence of the hospital was unbearable, so I turned over, got in my wheelchair (ignoring Heather's words), and shuffled through the records I had. One caught my eye. It was hand-decorated in a galaxy look with moons and stars shimmering against the light. I flipped it over to find a post-it note:

PAIGE'S SLEEPY TIME PLAYLIST. Too quiet? Figured at some point you'd need this to help you sleep. Enjoy, and get some shut-eye.

What I Didn't See Before

I felt the sides of my mouth curling into a smile. I put on the record, lowered the volume, shut off the lamp, closed my eyes, and drifted into a peaceful sleep.

What I Didn't See Before

Chapter 8
Paige
June 4, 2019

The morning dragged on forever, just like the three other mornings I'd spent in here. I had an aching in my bones and I was as uncomfortable as ever. I sat up and waited for the stars to vanish and then walked to my laptop. When I get sick with a virus I spend most of my time binge-watching Netflix, writing stories, or browsing YouTube and finding new people to watch. Usually, I get a few texts from my friends and once in a while will get a facetime from Joey, but I've heard nothing today. It was unusual, but then again, it's only 11:28 am.

    My daily routine usually starts with me ordering from room service. The food here is actually decent, but the coffee is even better. Lucky for me we have a Starbucks

What I Didn't See Before

and Dunkin' Donuts in our building. Since I woke up late this morning I decided to get some lunch. My all-time favorite is the grilled chicken fingers with honey mustard. I cannot explain how good these are for hospital chicken. Saint Andrew's Hospital is the only hospital food I can tolerate. The food at the other locations I was at before I came here tasted like it was intended for a dog. *Not* good.

    I ordered spinach and mint juice and a small caramel iced latte with my lunch. I know what you're thinking. *Spinach and mint juice? Gross!* That was my initial reaction too. It's not amazing, but it's super helpful to keep my iron levels regular. If they get too low it can be major trouble. I also made sure to have some sent to Kylee's room. Once in a while I'll send her little snacks as reminders to make sure her iron levels are stable. Since she's more fragile than the rest of the leukemia patients, I feel it is my responsibility to do my part to keep her healthy. Once in a while though, we will sneak out and do something for ourselves. Like last night. I made her get out of her room and come clean with me. Sometimes it's good for us to get up and move.

What I Didn't See Before

I was just finishing up lunch and scrolling through YouTube when I heard my phone buzzing. It was Joey calling me, finally.

"What took you so long?" I said jokingly.

"Paige, are you okay?" he asked in a panic.

"Woah, woah, yes, I'm fine. I'm just resting, relax."

"When did you last see Kylee?"

"A few nights ago. We cleaned the teen room together, why?"

"She's sick Paige, really sick."

Heather came rushing into my room in a full-blown panic. I had only pushed the nurse button a few seconds ago and she was already here.

"What's wrong?" she said out of breath.

"Kylee. What's going on with her Heather?"

"How do you know?"

"Joey called me. How serious is it?"

"Pneumonia. I didn't want to worry you, Paige."

"Pneumonia?" I choked out, my voice cracking and shaking. "Where is she?"

"Room 206. She's not conscious right now, but the team is taking good care of her."

What I Didn't See Before

I rolled out of bed and grabbed a sweater and my mask.

"Paige, no. Stop it. Get back in bed and rest," Heather persisted, guarding the door.

"I need to see her, please Heather, please let me see her! This is my fault, I dragged her out of her room to come help me." I burst into tears, choking on my words. "She didn't look like she was feeling good but I pretended not to notice, I thought she was just tired and this is all my fault. I made it worse!"

"Calm down. This is not your fault. She had the virus before then, but this means that you have it too, Paige. Going out to see Kylee right now means you might spread it to more people. I know that is not what you want. I will come in and check on you and give you updates on Kylee. But for now, please rest so you can get better. Please."

Heather's eyes were full of tears, but her face was serious. I softened, dropped my sweater and mask on the table, and crawled back into bed. She had a point. There was no good in me going to see Kylee.

"Thank you," she cracked, her face full of concern. "Let me check your temperature."

What I Didn't See Before

I had been up most of the night worrying about Kylee. It was now 2:52 a.m. and my sleep schedule was ruined. It had taken me a long time to get to bed at a decent time and stay asleep. It was the one accomplishment I can say I'm proud of. In fact, I helped all my friends perfect theirs. Oddly enough, my phone dinged. It was a text from a number I didn't recognize. All it said was, "Is this Paige?"

So I responded, "Yes, who is this?"

It was a few moments until another text came in. "It's Luca." I smiled, relieved to talk to someone after lying here for so long trying to sleep.

"Hi, Luca! How'd you get my number?" I replied.

"We had group therapy earlier today. I asked Kristina for it so I could see how you're doing."

"That was sweet. I'm doing okay, feeling better. No fever anymore."

"No fever? That's great! How much longer until you can leave your room?"

"I have to go 24 hours with no fever, so hopefully just today."

"Did they say what it was?"

"Pneumonia," I replied.

"Need any tissues?" he joked.

"Haha, no. I've got plenty here."

"We missed you today. It was my first time attending something with the group. They say in two weeks I should be out of my wheelchair and transferred to a walker."

"That quickly? That's awesome." I sighed, wondering what happened to him. I never had a chance to ask him, but maybe now was the time. "Can I ask you a question?"

"What's up?"

"What happened to you? Why are you here?"

The bubble went in and out for about five minutes until finally, his text came through.

"I made some bad decisions, Paige. I messed up. Before I explain, let me tell you why this happened. My dad is an alcoholic, barely present in my life. You would think I'd run from alcohol seeing what it does to my dad, but I did the complete opposite. That's what got me into this mess."

For a minute, my heart sank. Knowing this, maybe I would've told him about my dad the other day. The only person I can talk to about it is Joey, but let's face it, he can't

What I Didn't See Before

relate to me. His dad is his best bud, his role model, his partner in crime. Mine is just a blur buried in the darkest corners of my mind. I couldn't think of what to say to this, so I said the only thing that came to my mind. "I'm so sorry, Luca."

"No need to be sorry, my own mistakes got me here. Got into a drunk fight with my best friend, but the worst part is that I messed up my insides. Alcohol Gastritis is the whole reason that I'm here. Now everybody knows."

"Who? My friends?"

"Yeah. They had me share today at group therapy."

"Trust me when I say that those people are the most loyal, loving, and forgiving people I know. Your past isn't you. The present is what matters. Don't worry about them or me judging you, okay?"

"Okay. I won't."

"Good. Cause we have your back. Judgment free zone."

"Thanks, Paige," he replied.

I was just about to turn in for the night when I heard my phone buzz again.

"Your turn," he texted. "Why are you here?"

"Leukemia."

"That's cancer, right?"

"Yes, cancer of the blood."

"I had a feeling it was cancer but didn't want to make assumptions. I'm so sorry. What's that like?"

"It's a lot of fun," I joked.

"Oh yeah?"

"Yeah, you should try it sometime."

"Maybe I will," he joked back, sensing my sarcasm.

"There are good days and there are bad days. Staying here at Saint Andrew's has been helpful. I know if I kept transferring to and from home it would be too much on my body."

"That makes sense. Have you been progressing at all?"

"I don't really know. It's like I've been maintaining it for a long time."

"Do your friends also have cancer?"

"Kylee and Joey both have Leukemia like me. Eric has Multiple Myeloma and Kristina has Cystic Fibrosis. Most of the patients here have some type of cancer or chronic illness that can't be cured."

"I heard that Kylee is sick, does she have Pneumonia too?"

What I Didn't See Before

"Yes. Her chances are even lower than mine which is why I am so worried."

"I'm sorry, Paige. I can't imagine how scared you must feel."

I clenched my jaw, then my shoulders, following with the rest of my body until everything was clenched, and then I released. This always helps me calm down when my nerves strike.

"I am scared, really scared."

"I'm sorry for bringing it up."

"Don't be. All we can do for her right now is pray."

And with that last text, I rolled over to turn my *"Sleepy Time"* playlist on and fell asleep.

Chapter 9
Luca
June 5, 2019

It had been a while since I opened up to anyone, especially about my dad. It's always been difficult for me to talk about myself, especially to girls. I think the reason talking to Paige was so easy is because it was over text. If we had a serious conversation face to face, I'm honestly not sure how that would go. I tend to keep things bottled up inside and then try to drink it all away.

Being here and away from the party scene has been a good change for me. Meeting and hanging out with all of the patients here yesterday made me soften up a little bit and I actually made good friends with Joey. He and I don't exactly have a lot in common, but we do share interests. We both like French fries with extra vinegar, we love the show *Friends,* and we love to go skiing. He and I agreed that when we get out of here we will go skiing together at Peak Pike.

    The one person I've been dying to get to know more though, is Paige. There is something different about her, but something familiar. I can't quite pinpoint what it is, but she has something I want.

    Two quick and sharp knocks sounded at my door. Heather walked in, smiled at me, and whipped out her clipboard.

    "Morning Luca," she sighed. "Busy schedule for you today. Hope you slept well. Order some breakfast when you can. At ten-thirty you have your first round of physical therapy. At twelve o'clock, eat some lunch or a quick snack. At twelve-thirty you have occupational therapy with everyone. Two o'clock is yoga. I know that's gonna be hard for you since you're in a wheelchair, but we'll have you sit on the ground and at least do your best. At three-thirty a guest speaker is coming in to talk about her experience here, all of the kids are going."

    "Paige too?" I asked.

    She sensed the odd excitement in my tone and furrowed her eyebrows. "No, not today. Tomorrow she'll be with us, alright hun?"

What I Didn't See Before

"Okay, continue."

"Four forty-five is activity. I think you're all making some sort of drawings for the hallway outside of the teen room. Dr. Donald insisted on making it a bit more colorful. Six o'clock is dinner, seven o'clock is your second round of PT, and eight-fifteen to nine-fifteen is hang out in the teen room. You can go or you can come back to your room and relax."

"Sounds like a good day," I said smiling.

"You warming up here yet?"

"I think so. I really think I am."

Physical therapy was a little bit intimidating today. They brought out these two bars and placed me in the middle, then tried to help me stand. Because I've been in a wheelchair for a week, my legs were pretty shaky. They guided me with a belt to help my balance and I eventually got the hang of it. They've also been weaning me off of the numbing medicine so I've been able to feel more. Only problem I've noticed is that every single time I stand, I'm dizzy. I'm just assuming this has to do with me sitting down most of the time. Anyways, physical therapy is what's going to get me back on my feet.

What I Didn't See Before

The dizziness hasn't really been the only thing, though. There has been a strong, burning sensation in my chest. I figured this is due to the alcoholic gastritis and poisoning and all, but I thought that would have been a little more manageable by now. I guess I'll just have to keep on learning patience in this process.

I glance up at the ceiling in the lobby to see a huge golden chandelier. It was glimmering in the sunshine from the windows surrounding it, and ever so slightly rocking back and forth. Joey is on his way to meet me here so we can swing by Donald's office to check up on Kylee's progress. Although I don't know Kylee that well, I know she is important to everybody here. I want her to get better, so if there is anything I can do, I want to help. I know that if it were Alaina who was unconscious and sick I'd do anything I could to help. I've learned it should be the same for anybody.

"Big dawg!" I hear Joey shout from the elevator opening about 50 feet behind me.

"What's up," I say back.

"We gotta hurry if we wanna get back for OT. I'll push you, that 'ight?"

"Yeah that's cool." He spun my chair around and we began walking to Donald's office.

"Progress in PT?"

"Tried standing up for 40 seconds today."

"Did you fall?"

"Nope. Stood the full 40 seconds."

"Then don't say you tried. Say you did. Give yourself some credit." Joey patted me on the shoulder.

"Okay, I stood up for 40 seconds today without falling and I'm 100 percent positive I'll do it again tomorrow."

"Now don't get too cocky," Joey said jokingly.

I returned the banter with, "Did you put a whole bottle of gel in your hair this morning? Sheesh, dude. Go easy on it will you?"

Joey laughed. "Hey, I did exactly what the label said! Two pumps!"

"More like two bottles."

He and I laughed as we turned the corner to Donald's office. But he wasn't there. We asked a couple nurses where he was but nobody knew for sure, until we saw Dr. Huffman on the phone. Her face was red and she was trying to talk calmly. Joey and I tried to listen in but it

What I Didn't See Before

was hard to hear. We heard her say, "Please come as soon as you can," but that was it. We both knew this conversation had to be about something very serious, so we decided to walk away and head to OT.

After OT we headed to lunch. Kristina was stuffing a fluff and peanut butter sandwich down her throat when she caught me watching her.

"What is it?" she said with her mouth full.

"What does fluff taste like?" I asked curiously.

"Yeah," a girl named Emily chimed in. "I've never had it before."

"Come to think of it, neither have I," Joey said.

Kristina set down the sandwich and began to rip off big pieces for everyone. Before we ate the sandwich, she held up her hand demandingly.

"Don't eat yet. Let's all go around and say what's on our hearts." I almost had to hold in laughter when she said this. *Are we really doing a toast with a piece of fluff smothered bread?* But then Joey spoke.

"I want Kylee to be okay and for her to come back. I want Paige back here too. But, I'm glad to have Luca join our group." Joey turned to look at me and nodded his head, signaling it was my turn.

"Uh, I'm glad to be here. It's, um, well, it's ten times better than being at, um..." I looked away quickly, hoping the next person would jump in with their toast. Instead, there was an awkward silence. I looked up to see the group staring at something behind me. Puzzled, I turned around to see what was going on. Right then my heart dropped. Donald was pushing a stretcher with a sheet over the body.

"This can't be real," Joey cried. "I just saw her laughing and enjoying life just a few days ago. Why do things like this happen? Why do good people always end up with cancer? Why do good people have to die?"

"I know Joey, Kylee was a really amazing person."

"Stop it, Luca. You barely knew her. You don't have a right to pretend like you're in excruciating emotional pain over someone you've only known for like, a week! Do you know how much this hurts? To have someone you love pass away? To not even be able to say goodbye to them?" Joey's voice softened. He slammed his hand against the table repeatedly and then dropped his face into his hands.

What I Didn't See Before

"I lost my mom," I choked out. Joey lifted his head slowly and turned towards me.

"You did?"

"I was eight. My dad got remarried to the lady who is now my step-mom. My mom was a great woman but she had bipolar disorder. She ended up committing suicide. I miss her every day."

"So did my mom." Joey wiped his teary eyes, full of regret and sorrow.

I haven't told many people about my mom. It's one of the most difficult things for me to talk about, above all other things. One of the reasons I resent my dad so much is because he never stepped up and acted like a real parent should. Even before my mom passed away he never tried to make us feel important. My step-mom is a wonderful person. I can't help but wonder why she's with my dad.

"Are you okay?" I asked. "Like, do you miss her?"

"Yeah, every day. But it was her time, I guess. You?"

"I do. I always wonder what my life would be like if my dad had died instead of my mom. Sometimes I wish that were true."

"Why?"

What I Didn't See Before

"I don't want him dead, I just-"

Suddenly I'm cut off by Paige bursting through the cafeteria doors. She's dragging her IV stand, Fred, behind her and limping/running towards Joey and me.

"No no no no!" Paige held her hands to her mouth. "Joey, please tell me it's not true. Please tell me it's not true, please! Please, Joey, this can't be happening, she can't be dead Joey she just can't! She can't!"

Paige threw herself into Joey's arms and started sobbing. She was sobbing harder than I've ever seen anybody cry. Her lungs were desperate for air and she wheezed every time she inhaled.

I used to think I was heartless. When people cried I would laugh. I was always annoyed by the sound of crying. I thought if you cried you were weak. But seeing Paige in this state shattered every single piece of me. All I want to do is pull her in and hold her tight until she feels better. But even I know this is an inappropriate time to do this, so instead I just sit back with my arms crossed in front of my chest and watch Joey comfort her.

"Hey, you okay?" I text Paige. I don't even know if she'll respond. I know she's going through a lot right now

What I Didn't See Before

and it's going to take time. Joey's right, I didn't know Kylee that long, which means I really haven't known anybody here that long. I don't know their story. But I want to. It's taken me a long time to open up and talk to other people and I'm certainly not going to let that streak I'm on right now die.

My mom stopped in earlier today to talk to me for a while. She asked how I have been holding up here, what it's been like, and if I've made any friends. I told her all about what's happened in the time I've been here, and about Kylee. She talked to me about how things were back home with Alaina, and about dad. Apparently I've missed a lot, including Mazin coming by to see if I was okay. My mom explained to him I was in the hospital having the time of my life and that Mazin told her he'd stop over sometime soon.

Honestly, I was a little surprised. After what happened I didn't think any of my friends would want to stick around. I've always been the guy to start fights and take things too far, especially when under the influence. The fact that I have an old friend who actually cares to stick around after what happened is mind boggling.

What I Didn't See Before

Mazin and I have been friends since the 8th grade, the year life went downhill. He was the one who smacked the first bottle of whiskey out of my hand when I tried to sneak it. He was the first one who talked some sense into me after I tried to start a fight with Brad Ruggley. I still think it would've been fair to fight him, though. After all, he did call my sister fat. I was only trying to defend her.

After my mom died, my sister started forming an eating disorder. She would binge every time she thought about the pain of losing her. It was a vicious cycle, always eating and throwing up, eating and watching television, eating and sleeping. It took her two years to realize that lifestyle just wasn't going to work. She started to exercise, eat healthier, journal, and read her Bible. Alaina is someone I look up to, even though technically she's younger than me.

I've never really gotten into my faith. Alaina is always talking about how amazing it is to be set free and follow Jesus. I used to go to church with mom and dad, but I haven't gone since I was eight. However, I always wonder if it would be any different now. Before, I never really tried to pay attention in church and I definitely didn't care about learning. Alaina is such a joyful and giving spirit though- I want to learn her secrets.

Even though all of these things are flooding my mind, I can't help but think about Paige and the way she was crying earlier. I want her to be okay. I really want to help her. The friendship between her and Joey is very strong and I just need to make sure I don't get in the way of that. To be honest, I don't know how long I'm going to be in this place. It could be a little while longer, or it could be much longer. All I know is that I'm going to need some expert advice if I want to help Paige.

What I Didn't See Before

Chapter 10
Paige
June 6, 2019

"Eric?" I blinked my eyes twice to see if it was really him. It had been so long since I saw him last. I remember the day vividly. We had the whole group come into his room before his stem cell transplant to pray for him. Each one of us laid a hand on him while Heather led us in prayer. It was such an emotional day for us all, especially Kylee. Eric was Kylee's "Joey". They had such a close relationship and never left each other's sides. I always dreamed the two would get married and run off to Greece to spend their lives together, happy and healthy. Now, well now it's all a mess. I wish more than anything that I could make something like that happen. Everything is broken.

What I Didn't See Before

But yes, it's Eric. His eyes have massive bags under them and he is skinnier than ever. "Oh my goodness, Eric it's really you!" I cry. I can't help it. The emotions are all pouring out of me at this point. I run up to him and squeeze him as hard as I can.

"It's good to see you, Paige." He smiles.

"It's really good to see you too. I just wish it didn't have to be under these circumstances."

"I can't believe she's really gone. My best friend is gone and I didn't even get to say goodbye. I had no idea it was this bad."

"It happened so fast. She was fine until she wasn't. It just doesn't feel real. I keep thinking she's just going to come back and everything is going to be okay." I looked up at Eric who was violently shaking, his face as pale as ever. "Are you okay?"

Eric cleared his throat and stared at the ground, his gaze transfixed on a single speck of mud on the doormat to the courtyard doors. "My transplant was unsuccessful."

This took me a minute to digest, until it hit me. Eric's cancer was spreading rapidly before his transplant and they needed to fix it. They had one shot, and now Eric is here in front of me saying it was unsuccessful.

"What? What do you mean it was unsuccessful?"

"I mean it failed, Paige," He took a deep inhale and said exactly what I didn't want to hear. "I'm terminal."

It all makes sense now. This is why he shut us out. This is why he's stayed in his room for two whole months just counting down his days until it was time to say goodbye. This is why every single time we tried to reach out to him he never responded. Everything's adding up, but everything is falling apart.

"How… how long do you have?" My eyes are full of tears again, my gaze transfixed on the same speck of mud as him.

"Five days."

"Five?" I cried.

"Five."

"Eric…"

"You don't have to say anything, Paige. I've come to terms with it but it doesn't feel real. All of this feels like a dream. I keep thinking I'm going to wake up and it's all going to be better. I'll be back home with my mom and my sister and we'll be playing make believe games just to make my sister happy. I want that so much, but there's nothing I can do to stop this from happening."

"You'll be in a much better and happier place," I say, placing my hand on his shoulder.

"How do you know?"

"The only way you'll make it there is if you believe you will. If you believe that Jesus is in your life and that he died for you. That he can turn your life around. That he's your savior forever." I smiled.

Eric took a minute to process this and then began to tremble.

"I do. I do believe. I've just never said it out loud before and I feel like it's too late, or I've missed my chance."

"No," I say, crouching down to meet his gaze. "It's never too late. That's the beauty of Him. He accepts and forgives at any time, no matter if it's the very last words you ever speak in your life. As long as you say it and believe it, that's all that matters. You know, Kylee was one of the most devoted people I've ever known. She would make time every day to take in God's word. She was always listening to sermons. Every time we went to the gym she'd have her headphones on playing some podcast by Jeremy Johnson. He was her favorite. Even in the worst moments of her life she kept on believing. And now I have full faith in knowing she's up there in Heaven with Him."

"I want to be there. I want to spend my life in eternity with Jesus," he said, looking up at me. "I know He's real. I've seen what He's done in my mom's life and I've seen what He's done in mine. He's given me so many undeserved blessings and I didn't even have to ask for them. He's been so good to me. I can say that even though I'm about to die, He's been so good. Throughout this struggle He's given me a purpose when I never thought I'd have one. I want to be with Him. I want to see Kylee up there, dancing and twirling without crumbling because of her frail limbs. I want to see all of Heaven rejoicing and singing. He's real, I know he is."

Eric's words began to resonate with me strongly. So many times in my life I've just gone through the motions and kept my relationship with Jesus under the rug. I always feel like mentioning His name would turn some people away from me, and I never wanted that. I've always wanted to be the person people could come and talk to regardless of their beliefs. Maybe I've been doing this all wrong. Maybe my purpose isn't to be everybody's friend, but instead to spread His love to the world and everyone I know. Some may accept it and some may not, but it's up to me to start that snowball effect.

"He is. He's real and if you believe that, tell Him. Tell Him you want him as your Lord and Savior. Tell Him all of the things you've said to me. I know He will forgive you and make you whole. All you have to do is tell Him. Salvation is right at your fingertips."

At this response, Eric closed his eyes and began to pray, accepting Jesus into his heart. I couldn't help but watch this amazing event I got to witness.

Joey and I walked in the courtyard for an hour, just back and forth discussing our feelings about this past week. Joey has always been super vulnerable and sensitive. Most of the boys I meet try and put on that "macho" attitude and don't discuss how they really feel. It's always driven me crazy, I mean, really, who wants to talk to a blank wall? No emotions, no feelings, nothing but words out of their mouths like "yeah" and "okay" and "cool". But I also don't like the dramatic type that cries at everything they hear or see. Especially the ones who can't handle it when you're just simply not interested in them. So, I guess a middle ground is what I look for. Joey is exactly that, middle ground.

He and I are the type of friends who have never had feelings for each other and probably never will. We're just too close for that. I always hear the saying, "marry your best friend", but that won't happen here. Joey has had plenty of discussions with me about his interest in other girls, mostly that he finds on social media since we only really have a social life here at the hospital. We joke about it a lot, the fact that neither of us will probably ever end up with anybody since we spend all of our time here.

However, there is something interesting about Luca that I can't figure out yet. He's confusing, and for some reason that intrigues me. He doesn't talk a lot about his personal life except for that one time, but since that talk we haven't texted at all. I don't know if he's waiting for me to text first or if he just doesn't want to talk at all.

"What do you think about Luca?" I suddenly blurt out.

"What do you mean?" Joey replies.

"I don't know, like, do you like him? Think he's a good guy?"

What I Didn't See Before

Joey turns his head to face me. He smiles and starts poking me. "Someone got a crush on the new boy, eh?"

"No," I laugh. "No, I wouldn't say a crush. Maybe like, curiosity?"

"You know what they say, G. Curiosity killed the cat. Don't be the cat."

"I'm not gonna do anything if that's what you're implying. I'm just interested. He seems like a good person but covers it up, almost like an act."

"Well, why don't you get to know him better? He probably would like you back if you made a move."

"I don't like him."

"Whatever you say."

"Don't say anything to him about this conversation, alright?" I point a finger at Joey dangerously.

"I'm just saying, every time you do that it's really not intimidating. You're like, 4'9."

"I'm 5'2!"

"Same difference!"

I rolled my eyes at him.

"But okay, I won't say anything." Joey grabbed my finger and locked his hand in mine and we walked back into the building together.

What I Didn't See Before

It's late now, around midnight. After what happened with Eric I realize my days are numbered and I really want to spend my time learning more about Jesus. So for the past three hours I've had my nose all up in the Gospel. Currently I'm spending my time reading Matthew, that way I can start at the beginning of the New Testament and make my way through the four Gospels. I want to read the Bible from cover to cover, but I really don't want to do it alone. I'd love to have someone to study with and read with. I really believe two brains are better than one.

My phone buzzes across the room. I walk over, grab it, and turn it over.

"Paige? You up?"

"Yeah," I reply. "You okay?"

"Yes. You?" Luca responds.

"I've been better. But I'm okay."

"I'm sorry. Anything I can do?"

"No, but that's sweet of you to ask. I'll be okay."

"What're you doing?"

"I'm reading, what about you?"

"What're you reading? Anything good?"

"Matthew, in the Bible," I say, hoping maybe he will resonate with this and say something like, "No way! I just read that a week ago!" I know the chances of that happening are very slim, but there's just something about him that I am intrigued by. I don't mean to hold high expectations or anything like that, but truly, I want to know more.

"Oh, are you religious?"

"No, I don't like to call it a religion. I'm a Christian, but it's more a relationship than religion. It's personal."

"Oh, sorry, we don't have to talk about it."

"No, L.O.L," I type. "I don't mean that. I mean my relationship with Him is personal. Like, I have a personal relationship with Him. I get to talk to Him about my life and He listens and answers me."

"He speaks to you?"

"Sort of. Not in a voice though. He speaks to me in other ways such as nature, through other people, in scripture, music, and more. If that makes sense."

"My sister is really into her faith. I've never really been around the people who care about it so I've never cared. Everyone who starts that relationship with Him though has this quality that I don't know how to describe, but I want it. I just don't understand it."

"That's okay. I don't understand all of it myself either. But hey, you want it?"

"I think so."

"How about this? Let me know if this is not your style. I want to read the Bible cover to cover. Would you maybe want to do it together?"

The chat bubble sat there for the longest time and then disappeared. It did this for a while, disappeared then reappeared. *Oh no, did I spring too much on him? I mean, this is all new for me too and I don't want to scare him off. It was just an idea and now I've scared him away.* My mind was racing and racing as I stared at the chat bubble going in and out and in and out. Scaring him is not what I'm aiming for. But really, there's no better time to learn about Jesus than in a hospital, surrounded by the smell of sanitizer and the aesthetic of lonely white walls.

Suddenly an answer appears. "Sure."

"Really?" I reply, almost a little too excitedly and a little too quick.

"Yeah, actually I think that's a great idea."

What I Didn't See Before

"Tomorrow, want to meet in the courtyard during lunch?"

"You can count on it," he replies with a winky face.

My heart started to race a little bit, pumping louder and louder. I smiled, holding myself back from jumping up and down, and said a quick "thank you" to the Father.

Chapter 11
Luca
June 7, 2019

Paige seemed so excited at the thought of us hanging out together that I had to say yes even though I don't quite understand what we're doing. I really only agreed to it because it gives me time to spend with her and we'll get to know each other better. I wanna be there for her next time something happens to her. I want to be the first one she sees and the first person she goes to for comfort. I'm still on the lookout for that expert advice on how to treat other people, that way I know how to treat Paige.

    My clothes have been huge on me recently. I've lost a lot of weight. I figured this would happen to me, you know, not being able to eat a lot and all. All of my muscle has basically faded away. When I look in the mirror I see a thin layer of skin and visible bones showing through. I felt like I was becoming stronger in physical therapy, but something doesn't add up. My body doesn't look right.

Alaina decided to stop by this morning and bring over some candles for my room. She's always been super generous without anybody asking her to be. But I guess that's kind of the whole point of generosity anyway, giving without asking or expecting to receive. She brought me a cinnamon roll candle, a watermelon fizz candle, and a mahogany candle. I lit the mahogany one because I know if I lit the other two I'd want to eat something and right now it's still too painful to try.

"So what's life been like here since I last saw you?" Alaina asked.

"A girl died, a boy is about to die, and Paige and I are hanging out."

"That's a lot. Who died?"

"Kylee, you met her I think."

"Oh no, yeah I did meet her. She and I tried to get you and Paige together. Oh my goodness, that's awful... she was so sweet. Do you know if she was saved?"

"I don't know."

"You don't know anything." Alaina rolled her eyes at me and then changed the subject. "So you and Paige are hanging out, huh? And I didn't even have to step in this time?"

"You didn't have to step in in the first place."

"I know, but I'm just that giving." Alaina smirked at me and lowered her gaze, meaning I should go on about our plans.

"We're just going to meet up at lunch and read a little."

"Pff!" Alaina scoffed. "You're going to read? Something other than the four books on your shelf? What book are you reading?"

"Well, Paige suggested that we read the, you know, the Bible."

"Wait, you mean to tell me that you, Luca Matthews, are going to read the Bible? I thought you never really cared about that stuff."

"She got all excited and I wanna hang out with her so I said yes."

"Oh, now that's pathetic," Alaina said, turning around in her chair to face the other direction. She stood up and began to walk around the room, pacing back and forth which is typically what she does before she starts yelling.

"What did I say?" I asked.

"Nothing!" she screamed. "You said nothing."

"Well, okay then-"

"Do you know for two years I've been praying you'd at least care a little about God? That you'd at least be the slightest bit interested in learning about the One who made you? And then I hear the only reason you're going to even touch the Bible is because of a girl. I mean, come on! It's just not at all right. You've probably got Paige thinking she's finally found someone else who, who wants to learn about Him. Finally someone else who doesn't care about earthly things. But no, that's not the case here. All you care about is the fact that you get to hang out with a girl. I just hope you pay attention to what you're reading, Luca. If anything I just hope that you'll do that."

Suddenly, Alaina grabbed her purse and her keys, slammed the door and left.

Well, she knows how to make quite an exit.

All of a sudden there was a knock at my door, a slow and curious knock. "Come in," I said.

What I Didn't See Before

Joey opened the door and gave me a quick smile before turning around to close it. "What was that all about?" he said, pointing to the door.

"My sister, she's just in a bad mood. What's up? Hanging in there?"

"Yeah, doing okay actually. I came to get you. Eric is having a mini celebration today and he invited you."

"Oh, okay." Suddenly I was caught off guard by the word "celebration". *Wasn't he about to die? What could he possibly be celebrating?* "What's the celebration for?"

"Four more days until Heaven," Joey said, punching my shoulder. He walked over and grabbed some shoes for me, one of my fancier pairs. "You're gonna need something a little fancier than what you have on."

"Well, what should I wear?"

"Hold on," Joey said, running back out into the hallway. It was a few moments before he returned. This time with Paige.

"Hey," she said, smiling.

"Oh, hey Paige."

"I heard you needed a little help picking out an outfit for today. Thankfully you've got me, I can throw something together. He has a nice wardrobe, doesn't he Joey?" Paige said, turning to him.

"Yeah, real nice," Joey said, shrugging and laughing.

"Well, gee thanks Joey. And hey, you can borrow my clothes anytime you want. Just say the word and I'm there for ya'," I said joining in on the fun.

"I might just take you up on that offer. Say, do you have any knee high white socks? Or a shirt with Britney Spears' face on it? That'll look real good on me."

"Hey," Paige said in a demanding tone. "Don't pretend to not care about the little things, like clothes. You could be unlucky and only own some lousy potato sacks for clothes."

"Yeah, you tell him Paige," I said, elbowing Joey.

Paige turned to me and smirked. "You too, charmer boy."

I know she was saying that to throw me off, and it worked. I think Paige was actually flirting with me. I wanted to play it safe and not get too excited over the fact that a really good girl for the first time in forever wanted to get to know me. I don't want to overshoot, but I also don't want to undershoot, if that's even a word.

What I Didn't See Before

Maybe Alaina was right. Maybe Paige is starting to flirt with me because she thinks I'm in it for God, or whatever. I'm not really, I'm really only in it for her, and maybe I'm wrong, but the only way I'll admit I'm wrong is if something miraculous happens to change my mind. I get my sister wanting me to go to Heaven someday, but I can't help the fact that I just don't understand the concept of it. Evolution is the only thing I really know.

"I'm a little confused," I say, looking up at Paige and Joey.

"About?" Paige asks.

"Celebration? Eric is about to die and he's throwing a party?"

"Well, you see," Paige responds, ducking down in front of my wheelchair. "Sometimes we have to make the best of what we've got. He could choose to live his last four days sulking if he really wanted to. But when you've got the joy of the Lord in you, that's the last thing you wanna do. He's excited."

"Listen," Joey cuts in. "We're not saying we're happy about this. Eric is one of our best friends and to lose another person this week is more than I can process right now. But Paige is right. Eric is one of a kind. He wants to

What I Didn't See Before

celebrate that he's going to Heaven now, and I think it's best we respect his wishes. Right?"

"Yeah, right."

At my response, Paige looks slightly disappointed and frowns a little.

"You okay?" she asks.

"Oh, me? I'm good. It'll be cool to see this, um, celebration thingy."

"Well if that wasn't the most untrue thing I've ever heard," Paige said and raised her eyebrows. She stood up. "Maybe this will cheer you up a bit."

I watched as Paige walked over to the record player in my room. She has such grace when she moves, such elegance. It's as if I'm actually watching the calm winds blow by the lakeshore back at home. They've come to life, something I've never seen before.

As I suspected, Paige turned on The Beatles and we sang as we got ready for Eric's celebration. I'm not used to having this much fun with a group of people and not having alcohol involved. Usually that's what it takes to loosen me up and to get me to have a good time. It doesn't work like this here. I could complain about being in pain, not being able to eat, and only being able to take sponge baths but

What I Didn't See Before

there's nothing but joy here- here with these two people, some music from an old record player, a hospital room, and nothing but water inside my bloodstream.

Approaching Eric's celebration was a little nostalgic for me. They actually set it up like a real party with streamers, a disco ball, loud music, and black lights. Donald and Heather had to be in charge of putting this together, nobody else here would take the time to make it look this fun and inviting. To my right, a huge table with snacks like chips, popcorn, cookies, brownies, and a punch bowl was screaming my name. It looked so good, I would actually kill to just take a bite of a warm, gooey, chocolate chip cookie. Fortunately for me, Paige is pushing my wheelchair so I have no way to go over there to grab one.

"Paige?" I look up at her and grin, a cheesy smile if I've ever felt one.

"Luca?" she says, returning the smile.

"How bad would it be for me to eat a cookie right now?"

"Do you want this to be a celebration for both you and Eric?"

What I Didn't See Before

I try to hold back a laugh, but it's inevitable. I almost feel bad for laughing, but I've always had trouble holding back my laughter at dark jokes. Paige starts laughing too, and her smile completely catches me off guard. The way her face lights up, her teeth so perfectly in line, her dimples that make her cheeks round, and her eyes that squint so tightly you can't tell whether they're open or not.

"Donald and Heather seem awfully close," I say, pointing to the two of them who are laughing and innocently touching one another.

"Secret time," Paige says, pulling me to the corner of the room. "For two years I've been trying to get those two together. Look how good they'd be for each other! Donald is in his twenties and so is Heather, they both work at the same place, both have really similar values. It's inevitable."

"I thought Heather was married?"

"Divorced. It was about four years ago. She still came to work every day with a smile on her face and put her feelings aside. When I first got here she could barely talk about it with me, she was still healing. She's not all that good with opening up about deep stuff. Hey, she's kind of like you!" Paige elbowed my arm gently and smiled.

"I'll get there."

"I don't have any doubt in my mind that you will."

"So Donald doesn't have any kids then?"

"Nope, he doesn't. You wouldn't believe how often he talks about them though. Anytime he and I get put into a room together all we can talk about are babies."

"Seriously? A dude?"

"Yeah! A dude can like babies, what's wrong with that?"

"Nothing I just figured most dudes don't fantasize over babies as much as women do."

"Well, you're not wrong," Paige pulled back. "But he's one of the few. Plus, he's young and he probably wants to start a family. I think about my future family all the time!"

"You do?"

"Sure! Haven't you thought about it once or twice?"

"No, I don't think I have. What do you think about?"

"Well, I know my family is going to be built on the foundation of Jesus. First and foremost I'll find a husband who loves and puts Jesus first. Then we'll get married and stay married for about a year before having kids."

"Only a year?"

"Yeah. What's the hold up?"

"What's the rush?" I argue back.

"Okay, fine. It can go either way, that's your opinion. Anyways, before you went and interrupted me," Paige said sarcastically. I dropped my jaw and waved my hand to signal for her to continue. "Then I'll have three kids of my own and adopt two."

"You want five kids?"

"At least five kids."

"Why so many?"

"More people to tell the world about Jesus. And, the more the merrier, right?"

"Hey, if you say so."

"I just don't want to waste anything while I'm here. None of us are promised tomorrow. For all we know we could fall asleep tonight and not wake up here on Earth ever again. That's just one of the many reasons why I'm lucky to have Jesus, you know? The promise of eternity in Heaven, at peace all of the time with Him, never having to worry about my cancer. I'll be cancer free in Heaven!

Seriously! I don't know the last time when I didn't have cancer running through my blood… but I won't there. I just think that's the most wonderful thing."

Paige's words really caught me off guard. It felt like a trance I was sucked into for years suddenly just left my body. She was right, we aren't promised a tomorrow. I don't want to find myself wasting so much time here and not seeking the right things. I don't know exactly who Jesus is, but now there is some eagerness inside of me to figure this all out. I don't know enough to believe, but I want to.

"How do I learn more about Jesus?" I blurt out.

Paige smiled at me, and her eyes told me a story. They told me I'm going to be okay. They told me I'm meant to be here in this very moment. They told me that my past is not the person I truly am. They told me I have a purpose. They told me I am loved. And then she spoke.

"I was waiting for you to ask me that."

What I Didn't See Before

```
Chapter 12
   Paige
June 7, 2019
```

I spent most of the night talking on the phone with my mom, who I always share everything withI told her about Luca and how I felt a very strange connection with him as soon as he got here. I told her about Eric and how instead of mourning his time on Earth coming to an end he was celebrating his new and better life to come. I told her about the fact that Luca asked me how he could learn more about Jesus. The phone call consisted mostly of my loud mouth sputtering on and on and my Mom giving some *oh's* and *wow's* once in a while. She is my biggest cheerleader, but today I could tell something was off with her. Her voice was shaky and I could tell there was some stress and anxiety behind it. Eventually she hung up and told me she'd call me later, so I just let it go at that.

I picked up my phone and dialed Joey's number. He, as always, picked up right away.

"Hey, what're you doing?" I asked.

"Watching the big game, why?"

"Can you pause the big game and run downstairs to the gift shop with me?"

"If you'll buy me a pack of sour gummy worms," Joey teased.

"We'll see. Meet me by the elevators?"

"Done. Be there in a minute."

I hung up the phone, put on my shoes, and grabbed my purse. All day I had been trying to decide whether or not to go to the gift shop and get Luca a gift, but I decided it couldn't hurt to spend a little money. Luckily for me, my mom has been sending me fifty dollars of spending money every two weeks. Of course I'd like to get a job of my own if I could, but Mom offered to do this for me until I am healthy enough to get one.

As soon as I opened my door, I spotted Joey across the hall by the elevators. I could see him messing with the back of his neck, per usual.

What I Didn't See Before

"Knock it off, Joey!" I shouted down the hallway.

"Whoops." He noticed what he was doing and put his hand down. "What're we shopping for?"

"A gift for Luca."

"You're buying him a gift? Well, then you really better get me some gummy worms."

"I'm getting him a Bible."

"He doesn't already have one?" Joey asked.

"I figured he didn't. I could tell he didn't seem too interested at the idea of God so I didn't push. I was waiting for a sign that I could push. And, I got it."

"Oh yeah?"

"At Eric's party," I said, pushing the down button on the elevator. "He asked me how he could learn more about Jesus. And what better way than to read the actual words He said, right?"

"That is true. So you were right then."

"Right about what?"

"Right that he was more interested in the idea of you than anything else?"

"Well, I don't like to get cocky or anything but… I think so!"

"I could tell. I'm proud of you for doing this, Paige. I know Kylee would be too."

I could feel the backs of my eyes sting, so I squished them shut super tightly, flushing all the sadness back to where it belongs.

"What're you doing?" Joey laughed hysterically and smacked my elbow. I started to laugh too, thinking about how ridiculous I probably looked making that face.

"I was trying-"

"I think you're supposed to be on a toilet right now."

"Very funny, Joey." I punched him in the arm and laughed.

The gift shop was full of different kinds of trinkets, candies, cards, and hospital branded materials. Since the hospital is Christian based, the Bibles were easy to find. In fact, there was a whole section of devotional books, testimonial books, faith based bookmarks and mugs, pins, stickers, and lots of other stuff. I decided the NIV version was the best one to get for Luca. It was the only version I could fully understand when I started reading the bible. I was completely lost trying to read the King James version.

What I Didn't See Before

Seriously, with each chapter I read, my eyes glazed completely over.

A lot of people use the Bible and what it has to say to try and convince me to forgive my dad. In a way, I know they're right. Everything God's word has to say is true and I should listen to it, but something is holding me back from forgiving my dad. I just can't get to the point of actually forming the words let alone getting them out of my mouth. Joey has been encouraging me for a year now to at least try. But why should I forgive someone who made life miserable for my biggest supporter? Who left as soon as things got hard with me medically?

I know people say kids often blame themselves for their parents divorcing, but when I say this, it is actually true. My dad left my mom because of me. Because I got sick and he couldn't bear the burden of paying for my medical bills. Everything seemed to be going so well in their marriage. They seemed to have it all together and to be so in love. Brayden and I stayed home many times while Dad and Mom went on vacations together. They'd send us postcards from all around the world of them smiling together. They looked so happy. So, where else could it have gone wrong? All of the signs point back to me.

Once I got back to my room, I felt this tug on me to start journaling. So, I pull out my journal and open it up to a blank page. To be clear, when I start journaling I never know what I'm going to write about. I just start with an empty page, a full mind, and a ballpoint pen. My brain fills up with thousands of thoughts while I'm writing. Sometimes they're fictional and sometimes they aren't. I divided my journal into three sections so I can write exactly how I'm feeling.

The first is a story section. Once and awhile I enjoy writing long, drawn out stories that I form in my imagination when I'm busy daydreaming. Honestly, I could see myself doing it as a career. There's something so beautiful about being able to escape your own reality with a character you make up in your mind. They truly take you on a ride and distract you from the realities of daily life. Back in first grade I wrote a story about a dolphin girl who's fin was chopped off by a giant machine owned by the so-called "villain" dolphin. It swam alone searching for help when a nice, big, strong dolphin man came to the rescue. She was saved! My first grade teacher thought I had a gift right from the get go. She showed the principal my paper and read it to my class. During that time I thought I

What I Didn't See Before

was so cool. Writing has been that little sliver of hope for me since I was little, and even when I got sick.

The second part of my journal is the actual journaling section. Journaling for me has always been so therapeutic. I've never been good at getting my feelings out in words that actually make sense. I always seem to stumble over my emotions and put them in words that don't quite make any sense. Journaling is that one spot where it's okay if I don't make sense. It gives me a little release from feeling like I need to have everything together and know who I'm supposed to be, because I'm not quite there yet. In fact, I'm far from it. I've always leaned towards the guided journals because it's difficult for me to come up with prompts on my own. The guided journals at least give me a little sense as to what I should do to fix my current situation.

The third section is where I compose my own songs. I do this a lot, but I'm not the best singer so I never do anything with them. It's not so much about the rhyming or making much sense at all, it's more personal than that. It's actually very useful to me since I can't really put my emotions into words that truly make sense. My lyrics are more complex and diverse. They make you think quite a bit, even Joey has tried to analyze some of my lyrics and he couldn't do it.

Joey is a wonderful singer. He has a bit of that southern charm that most girls swoon over which makes his vocals all the more lovely. He writes his own music but he doesn't put any words to them, so actually we make quite the power duo when we put both of our brains together. He always tells me that he dreams of becoming a singer in Nashville, and I always encourage him to put his music out on the internet. I just know so many people would adore him and listen to his music.

Before it gets too late, the thought pops into my mind that I need to call my mom. I only really get to talk to her on the phone since she's so busy trying to provide for my little brother, herself, and me. The last time she came to the hospital was early spring. A lot of the kids here get to see their parents almost every day, but Joey and I have always been unique in that sense. Kristina's mom spends more time with her than we get to. We rarely see her anymore, her mom, dad, and cousins are always up here playing cards with her and cheering her up. I've gotten used to how things are now. Sure, I'd like to see my mom and brother more often, but they have responsibilities. Once my brother gets his car, I'm sure he will drive up here all the time to hang out with me.

The phone rings a couple of times and I'm sure she's not going to pick up, but she does.

"Honey?" Mom said.

"Mom?" Right off the bat, I can tell she's been crying. Her muffled sniffles over the phone are all too familiar.

"How are you?"

"I'm okay- Mom what's wrong?"

"I'm okay honey, I just need to talk to you about a few things and I know hearing them is not going to be easy for you."

"Okay," I said uneasily.

"Well you know how things have been hard around here lately and how I've not really felt like I've been able to stay on top of things."

"Uh-huh."

"Well, for the past two months I've been talking to someone who has been really helpful and made my life a lot easier. He's helped with the bills, he's helped make dinner and clean the house, he's helped take your brother to school."

"Mom! That's so great! Why would I be upset about that?"

"That someone is your father."

If I want to go back in time and journey all the way back to my childhood, I can do it in a split second. I was always a "Daddy's girl". He and I were like a tag team, an unstoppable duo, a double force. He brought me up and raised me to be a very polite girl, someone who respects all people no matter what their life looks like, and as someone who put Jesus in the center of it. He taught me how to play softball and coached my team for a year, which was the year before I started feeling sick. I was about seven at that time. I always tried to push down how I was feeling because I just wanted to play. My dad could always see right through my lies and kept my best interests at heart. He'd check my temperature and if it was a little higher than normal, he'd suggest we do a water chugging race and watch comedy movies. I'd always fall asleep because, well, I was sick. He'd cover me up with a blanket and place a kiss on my forehead, and stay there with me until I felt better.

What I Didn't See Before

My mom was always there for me too, but in a different way. She has always been more of the worrier. Anytime I felt any sort of pain, she'd be on the phone with my pediatrician. Although once and awhile I'd get annoyed with this, I also have a great amount of respect for her for doing so. It just showed that she really cares about me and doesn't want anything bad to happen to her "little girl".

But now, now I see my dad in a totally different light. I see him as the man who left when things got hard, as the man who only reached out once in a great while to see how we were doing. It's been four years now, and he's reached out as many times as I can count on one hand. And now my mom actually wants him back in our lives? All I can think about is how he's just going to do it again. He's just going to leave us empty handed again and not tell us the reason why. Nothing good can come of this, only more pain and sadness.

"What?" I stuttered.

"I knew how hard this was going to be for you and I honestly was afraid to tell you, but Paige, he's really sorry."

"I don't care if he's sorry, Mom! He left us!"

"I know honey, but listen-"

What I Didn't See Before

"No! I don't want to listen! Mom, I do not want him back! A real Dad would never do the things he did to our family. A good *husband* would never do those things."

"Paige, there's a reason for all of this."

"A reason for what?" I shrilled.

"For why he left and for why he's coming back."

"Oh, okay," I scoffed. "I'd love to hear it then. What's the reason then Mom? Huh?"

"Paige, I'm not saying you have to forgive him right now but-"

"Well good! Because it's been years and I still think about it every day. It's going to take a lot more than chores and rides to earn my trust and forgiveness."

"That's fine, Paige. You take your time. I just wanted you to know that this is happening. I didn't want to keep any secrets from you. I'm not forcing anything on you, but please just take some time to think about the big picture. He still needs to earn my trust back too. I get that and he needs to do the same for you and your brother. Brayden is not totally happy with him either, but he is getting a lot better. This is going to take time for us all. Just please don't let the past affect your future."

What I Didn't See Before

My mom tends to put words together in a way that makes everything seem like it's going to be okay. For a long time now she's been repeating the phrase "Your future doesn't depend on your past." I think pretty logically, so when prompted with this I'd respond, "But Mom, don't your past job experiences and your education affect your future career?"She'd respond with, "Only if you let it." I didn't really understand what that meant for a long time and I am still learning to this very day what it means. A human can change their minds at any time about what they want to do. Life is way more about the present than the past.

That's one very major reason why I've been following Jesus for a long time. He doesn't let our past affect our future or our relationship with Him. His mercies and His grace are renewed every single morning.

As for me, not so much. It's been years, and forgiving my dad has been put on the back burner and never spoken of unless I had to. Dr. Woods often pries it out of me any chance she gets, but I am pretty good at avoiding questioning. The fact that my mom, the woman who was left alone and had to go through so much to get back on track is willing to forgive him makes absolutely no sense to me. Maybe that's a really, really great thing for her, but I cannot see myself reciprocating.

"Okay, Mom. I'll try."

I hang up the phone and set it down. Although I'm not happy about any of this, I know she's right. I have to at least try to move past this and forgive him, but the truth is I have no idea how to begin.

Chapter 13
Luca
June 10, 2019

The past couple of days have gone by quicker than I could ever have imagined. The saying, "Time flies when you're having fun" is really resonating with me. Paige and I met up for our first Bible study two days ago. I never would have labeled myself a "deep thinker" or a "question asker", but the thoughts just kept on coming. When she handed me my Bible, I wasn't sure how to feel, but I knew to react kindly. It was an interesting moment, but it made me see just how caring Paige is.

I also never would have imagined that a drunken fight would get me to where I am right now. The weirdest part about all of this is that I don't miss the feeling of being drunk anymore. That feeling used to be the only reason I liked going to parties. It was an excuse to do those things, to feel like you're invincible, to feel less anxious, to feel uplifted and loose. Now it sounds really unappealing to me. I guess things you would never expect have a bigger impact than things you do expect.

  My mom came to visit me last night. I told her all about Paige and how she bought me a Bible, and about my physical therapy and how I've been making major progress. I've never seen her face light up as much as it did when I talked with her this morning. She's always been worried about me. As soon as she and my dad got married, I half expected her to show her true colors. I figured she was going to be done caring about me and start acting like my dad. Truth is, I have no idea what my Mom sees in my dad or why she chose to marry him. My mom is way too good a woman to be with a guy like him. I wonder if she saw his true colors before he married him, or if he hid them from her.

  Today is one of those days I wish I could be outside or doing something fun. Apparently it's visitor day so there are no classes or appointments. I texted Joey but he's spending the day with his brother. I texted Paige but her mom is visiting. She seemed pretty anxious about her mom coming in so I tried to spend as much time with her yesterday as I could to get her mind off whatever it is that's making her anxious. Even though that girl is such a chatterbox, she doesn't like to talk about what's bothering her. Every time I asked what's going on, she changed the subject. I know she and I haven't known each other forever, but I want to be someone she can talk to.

Before I can pull out my phone to text anybody else there is a knock at my door. "Come in," I say, confused as to who was coming to see me.

"Luca!" Mazin swings open the door with his hands up in the air.

"Dude!" I laugh and greet him with a hug. "What're you doing here, man?"

"I came to hang out with my bro, why else would I be here?"

The last time Mazin and I hung out was about four months ago. He and I used to be super close before I made friends with the worst group of boys at our school. He never really left or quit being friends with me, he just distanced himself for a while. I understand why now because I've had a lot of time to think, but I didn't really understand why before. To be fair, there are a lot of things I didn't really see before. I never saw that the things I was doing were wrong. I never saw that I was completely throwing my life away for a drink. I never saw that I was treating everyone in my life completely wrong and judging everyone's character before I even knew them. I never saw that my younger sister was begging for me to get help. All of these things and more were right in front of my eyes, yet I never saw them.

Mazin and I caught up for about an hour and a half. He told me how his college applications were going and that he was finally accepted into his dream school, Harvard. He's always been incredibly smart so it was no surprise to hear that he got in. Ever since we were in middle school he has been talking about criminal justice and how badly he wanted to study it. He was always checking out law related books from our school library and shoving his nose into them for hours upon hours. Anytime I tried to get his attention while he was reading he'd shush me and stick his index finger up in front of my face. I remember how that got on my nerves so much I actually started shoving his finger up my nose every time he did that. Mind you, we were in middle school, but nonetheless, gross, I know.

What I Didn't See Before

He has always been very serious about his education and he knows exactly what he wants to do with his life, so talking about his future career set off a huge red alarm in my brain. I have absolutely no clue what I want to be, and I just finished my senior year. I applied at a couple colleges but I haven't heard anything back from them yet, which also worries me. Everybody knows what they wanna do with their lives and I'm completely stuck with not even a single clue. People always tell me I have plenty of time to figure it out still, and that I can go in undecided. I've spent so much of my life worrying about other things that I never actually got to thinking about what's really important. Mazin also had the longest talk with me about his new girl Tabitha and how he thinks "she's the one." His life sounds like everything is falling into place, whereas mine isn't making much sense at all.

I would like to think that I found "the one" but it's hard to say. We both have our minds focused on so many things going on in life right now and I can't tell if it will go anywhere. Being here in this program the focus is on one main goal- getting better. It's not like we are taught anything about relationships. Plus, the schedule each day is

What I Didn't See Before

jam packed which makes it hard to see Paige as often as I'd like.

Although all of these things are clouding my mind, there is some silver lining. The program is actually working, and I sort of doubted it would. I wasn't expecting to hear the ways they teach us how to deal with pain. I had a feeling it was going to be this weird and complex medicated system with lots of dietary restrictions. However, that's not at all what it's been. It has actually been the complete opposite.

In fact, we tend to fill our evenings with fun games to get our mind off of the pain. Tonight's game was a scavenger hunt around the first floor of the hospital, including the parking garage. Joey got put on a separate team than Paige and I which made things quite interesting to say the least. I never thought of Joey as the competitive type, but boy was I wrong. I was so used to his friendly "Goooood morning everybody!" that I never saw this side of him coming.

We had a text message group chat going between the two teams to discuss anything important that happened, such as one of the teams finishing. One of the tasks on the list was to find a pamphlet in the parking garage. Our team was definitely winning at this point, but we were in a bit of a pickle. There was only one pamphlet. We took it anyway thinking maybe they could just opt out from that one. A couple minutes later a text appeared on my phone from Joey. "You snakes," he said. We all had a pretty good laugh about it later.

Besides the fun games and all, one of the things they ask of us is to not talk about our pain. Personally, it's been fairly easy to avoid, but when people ask it is near impossible. Anytime one of my family members call I have to immediately remind them not to ask me. It's been the hardest for my mom to call and not ask, "How are you feeling honey?" It's a reflex for parents and people that love you. But it's true. I've started to notice that not talking about it really helps. I've had more time to focus on more important things.

Recently though, something really weird has been going on with me. Every couple of hours I run to the bathroom nauseous. Once in a while I'll vomit up blood, which has been pretty scary. I'm assuming this has to do with being weaned off of all of the medication I was taking. Swallowing hurts a lot as well, worse than usual actually. In fact, that makes the dizziness so much worse. I thought maybe it was because I was dehydrated the first time it happened so I drank a ton of water and Gatorade thinking that would help. It didn't, though. It's as if my legs forgot what it feels like to be used. The dizziness was pretty bearable when I first started to feel it, but it feels like it's progressing.

Earlier today we said goodbye to Eric. It was hard, but his suffering painlessly faded away. Somehow he was still cheerful as he was going, excited to see the light of Heaven enter his vision. I believe we witnessed him seeing that light, because a few seconds before he took his last breath, he faintly smiled.

Heather entered my room this evening with a big smile on her face as she brought in my dinner, which made me wonder a little bit if this had anything to do with Donald. She's been giddier than ever lately and spending way more time with him. I always see the two of them sitting together during lunch break in the cafeteria, laughing and talking with one another. Paige is always talking about the two and how she wants to seal the deal between them. She's definitely a meddler in other people's business, but she does it tastefully.

"I brought your favorite, mac and cheese with ketchup!" Heather grins widely and sets up my table for me.

"Sounds great, thanks."

She takes a seat in the empty chair by the corner of the room and snacks on a granola bar.

"I'm on break," she says, clarifying herself. I nod at her. "How is everything going here in room 201?"

"Not too shabby. My strength definitely seems to be improving, which is great. Doing chores has gotten easier, exercising is getting there, and my sleeping schedule has gotten a lot easier."

"Well, don't you know just how to make my night? That's great. Was hoping to hear those things."

"Yeah," I say, thinking. I was planning on maybe telling Heather about all of these new symptoms I've been having, but she seems so happy with what I just said about things going so great that I changed the subject instead. "You know, you and Donald seem to be getting pretty close."

She blushes a little but tries to cover it by putting her hand to her forehead. "We're just good friends who work together."

"Yeah, sure. I'm sure that's all it is."

"It is! I mean, we both have responsibilities here and it makes it easier to talk to each other when we're both feeling overwhelmed with it all. We both care about all you kids so much. Sometimes we just need to sit back and have a good laugh with each other."

"Uh-huh. Sounds like flirting to me," I say taking a huge bite of my mac and cheese.

"This is unfair. I could be saying the same things about you and Paige you know."

"What about me and Paige?" I smirk and lean back into my bed.

A knock sounds at my door and Paige walks in, holding the leash of the hospital's rescue dog, Brody.

"Am I interrupting?" Paige says, eyeing the two of us.

"No," Heather says smiling. "I was just bringing him his dinner. You two have fun with Brody." Heather winked at me, and closed the door behind her.

"Well, hello there!" I slowly get off my bed, watching as the stars steal all of my vision away, my heart beating a hundred miles a minute. I duck down anyways to pet Brody, missing him by about two feet.

What I Didn't See Before

"Luca?" Paige says, worry punctuating her words.

"Hi, Paige." I look up, trying to find her with my eyes but desperately failing.

"You okay? I'm over here... What's wrong?"

At this point, it's just plain embarrassing. Her voice is fading into a blurry chaotic tunnel and my mind is fogged up completely. *Why does something like this happen to one of us every time we try to hang out? Why now? Why couldn't this just wait until I'm alone?* The darkness slowly takes over as I feel my body start to give out. I know what's about to happen. I feel for the ground and lay my cheek against the cold floor. Everything fades away, Paige's voice, Brody's kisses against my cheek, and the tornado my body is whirling through.

"Luca? Are you awake yet?"

I recognize Paige's voice as my eyes open and I stare at the bright fluorescent lights above me.

"I'm up," I whimper.

"You passed out."

"First you, now me." I laugh, trying to ease her anxiety, and mine because I do not feel right. "What're we gonna do about the two of us?"

Paige doesn't laugh. She leans into me, grabs my hand, and squeezes it. "Why didn't you tell me about this?"

"I'm sorry. I've just been trying really hard not to talk about my pain."

"I get it, but this is different. This is not your usual pain, this is serious. I'm worried about you, Luca."

I know that her being worried about me should mean something good to me, but it just makes me feel guilty. She already has so much going on and I do not want to be the cause of increasing her worrying.

"I was probably just dehydrated," I say, trying to divert the conversation.

Paige looks at me intensely, tears forming in her eyes. She squeezes my hand a little tighter and looks down at the ground nervously.

"Paige, what is it?"

She looks back up into my eyes, swallows, and takes a deep breath.

Just then, the doctor walks in, and breaks the news. "They did an endoscopy on you while you were asleep and found stage two cancer in your esophagus."

My heart dropped down to the bottom of my body.

What I Didn't See Before

Everything I have ever known about myself was reigning untrue. I've always been able to handle difficult news in a calm manner and with a smile on my face. But this, this was different. This is cancer. This is the disease I've seen too many good people suffer with. This is an evil too many undeserving people die from. The disease that puts life plans on hold and then makes you think there is hope to return to them but cancels them at the last second. I've watched movies about this disease with my parents and agonized as the little boy loses his fight to it. And now, now I have this disease inside me. I can't take some pills and watch it fade away. *How could I have not seen the signs? Why didn't I say something when I first started feeling weird?* First it was the burning sensation in my chest, then the dizziness, then the vomiting, then the swallowing.

"This is all my fault."

"What?" Paige shakes her head. "How can you say that? This is anything but your fault, Luca. Sometimes we are given battles that we just have to accept. You didn't do anything wrong."

"Yes I did. I'm here because of alcohol and now I have cancer because of alcohol. I could've controlled that."

"You need to let go of the past or you'll never be able to move on to better things that the future has for you."

"What if I don't have a future?" My voice is shaking at this point. My heart feels like it's going to explode into a thousand tiny pieces.

Paige's grip on my hand got tighter. "I know you do. Just trust me. You have a future."

What I Didn't See Before

Chapter 14
Paige
July 3, 2019

"A little to the right," I laughed, guiding Luca to pin the tail on the donkey. Once a month we do these childish games during teen night to help us feel a little less uptight and a little more at ease. As silly as it sounds, it seriously is one of our favorite nights of the month. We all laugh and have a good time playing them- especially duck duck goose. Why duck duck goose? Well, it's pretty fun to watch people chase each other around in their wheelchairs. Plus it helps the arms tone a little bit.

Ever since Luca was diagnosed with cancer, he's been acting different- different in a good way. It's like he wants to do everything and conquer everything despite his pain and symptoms. Seeing him open up to more people and dive deeper into God's word has been incredible to witness. He and Joey are becoming a lot closer which makes me happy. It's good for Joey to finally have another guy hanging around here. I could tell once in a while he got a little sick of all the girls wanting to do girly things together, but he didn't want to be left out so he tagged along. He has a major fear of missing out, but then again, I can relate.

    Luca and I are currently in the book of Numbers. We thought it would be fun to go from the very beginning of the Bible and work our way to the end. Although a lot of people frown upon doing this, we've actually had a lot of fun. It's an interesting way to watch the story unfold book by book, and also makes it clearer so we don't skip or miss anything. Numbers is all about God's chosen people, the Israelites, and their forty year-long journey to the promised land. Unfortunately, it's kind of a disaster. The people keep rebelling, worshipping other things, not trusting in God, and ultimately going their own way. Not everyone makes it to the promised land because of their own selfish reasons, but God still keeps his promise to the ones who believe and trust in Him.

What I Didn't See Before

In a way, this book kind of reminds me of modern day. God promises us eternity with him if we just believe and trust, but people decide to go on their own path all the time. Who wouldn't want the promise of peace and happiness eternally? I know I do, but some people don't understand it yet and it takes a lifetime to figure out. Sadly, some people don't figure it out at all. Still though, God never leaves anybody in the midst of doubt and uncertainty. Even when humanity shames Him, degrades Him, and mocks Him, He still loves us. I know for a fact I could never do that.

The last time I was in public school I remember a whole bunch of kids mocking me for my appearance. At the time, I was gaining a lot of weight due to chemotherapy. Nobody knew I was suffering from cancer. My hair started to fall out, my brain rarely ever worked to its full extent, and I even started to lose a few teeth. This just goes to show how much God loves us. I don't think I could ever have loved those girls who were making fun of me during that time. After my cancer started to progress and I had to be hospitalized, I was actually relieved that I didn't have to go back to school with those girls. When they found out I had cancer, their parents made them send me handwritten apology letters for bullying me. When I started to lose all my weight and got a wig, I wanted to go back to school just to show them how I looked now. That never happened though.

Now I see an opportunity to use my battle as a message rather than revenge against the people who made fun of me. I want to help other kids going through the same thing gain their confidence back, which is why if my cancer ever goes away I'd love to specialize in pediatric counseling for children with cancer. I've always loved working with children and being around them. They bring so much light into my life, a light I don't ever want to see fade away. I miss always being curious like a child. As often as I can, I try to do child-like things just to spark that curiosity in me, which is exactly why I love nights like these.

Luca pinned the tail right on the donkey and everyone cheered for him, congratulating him with high fives and pats on the back. He and I went back to sit down as the next pair went up to try and I could tell something was bothering him.

"Everything alright?" I asked him.

What I Didn't See Before

"Yeah, my shoulders are just super sore." He shrugged them up and down and tried to massage them a little bit.

"Sit in front of me. I'll help."

I grab his two shoulders and give them a massage to help with the pain. I'm proud of how he's been doing lately. He's been working extra hard during physical therapy and taking his radiation therapy very seriously. It's just a given that he's going to be super sore from all the hard work he's been up to. Even on days when he's at his worst, he's sticking to all of the program's protocols and trying to help anyone who has been struggling. His mood has been better than ever and he's been more invested in studying God's word. I'm not sure what exactly came over him, but I like it.

"What're you doing for dinner?" Luca turned around and looked at me.

"I was planning on ordering some room service."

"Yeah, cancel those plans. I have something better."

I raised my eyebrows, tilted my head, and smiled. "You have something better?"

Luca shifted his position to look at me, offended. "Yes. Why did you say that like you were shocked?"

What I Didn't See Before

"Sorry," I laughed. "I didn't mean it like that. I'm just surprised is all."

"Well, get used to it. I'll pick you up at 8:15. Bring a coat."

"Luca Matthews," I grinned. "Are you asking me out on a date?"

"If that's okay with you, then yes. Yes I am."

He smiled at me and turned back around to face the other direction, cheering on the other two people who pinned the tail on the donkey. I could see his side profile as he smiled at them. His smile is so charming. He's got these two little freckles right in the dimples of his cheeks which fold inwards every time he smiles. That smile is one of my favorite features about him. This newness and liveliness he has inside him is exciting. I don't know how to pinpoint what it is, but something definitely sparked it. This isn't random.

"Hey," Joey walked over to us and sat down next to Luca.

"My man!" Luca gave him a bro hug and patted him on the back. I watched as the two talked together, just thinking to myself about how crazy this past month had been. I've never been the type of girl to want a boyfriend

What I Didn't See Before

right now or even think about boys much. But now I feel myself falling for this boy. I may be young still, but I've had crushes before and it feels like so much more than that. I don't think it's love. I'm only seventeen and it just seems irrational to think I'd know what love feels like so soon, but it's definitely a strong feeling. I get excited to see him every morning and spend the day with him at the program working on getting better. I look forward to the times he and I get to be alone. And at the end of the night, when everyone goes to bed, I can't help but replay the day over in my head.

  Lucky for me, when my mom came to visit earlier today she didn't bring my dad along with her. She and I both know it's way too soon for me to try and deal with that, especially with everything that's happened here lately.

  I still think about Kylee every day and pray that she's living the dream up there. Eric's parents came to visit the kids about a week ago to talk to each and every one of us about his journey and how they were getting through everything together. They had a wonderful story to share and I just know they will be able to touch lives all around the world. In fact, they just started working on a book together about their testimony.

What I Didn't See Before

My brother tagged along with my mom today. He couldn't stop talking about my dad and how he's actually been happy that he's gotten to spend time with him. I can't blame him. Everything he was telling me that they did sounded exactly like what my dad and I used to do when I was a kid. When he was telling me this I felt myself gravitating towards my phone to text my Dad just to see how he was doing. My chicken self backed out at the last second though.

It was good to see my family again. I thought about telling them how close Luca and I were now and all the time we spent together, but instead I just introduced him as "the new kid in the program" Honestly, I don't know why it was hard for me to say that he was more than just the "new kid at the program". Joey seems to think it's that I didn't want to steal any of the thunder from my mom, you know, about her love life starting up again.

I had told all of my friends that my mom had a boyfriend now, but I don't have the courage to tell them that it's my dad. I know Joey would just encourage it and say it's great that they're back together and trying it again, but I don't really want to hear any of that. Dr. Stone has even asked multiple times during therapy if I liked my mom's new boyfriend and all I can say is "I'm not sure yet." I'm pretty sure she can sense something is going on there, but I try my best to pretend everything is fine.

"That's all I have for you guys today," Donald says. Then he clasps his hands together as if he is going to give a huge speech. "Oh, well, that's almost all I have for you guys." He looks to the back of the room where Heather is sitting in a soft and cozy blue chair drinking a cup of coffee. Donald signals her to come up to the front and winks at me.

Donald has been chatting with me back and forth about this very moment for about a month now. We all know that he and Heather have been an item for a while now and that they've been trying to keep it private and act like nothing is there. After I talked to Donald about this, he told me they'd been dating for a year and eight months. If anything, that shocked me the most. How could I have missed that? A year and eight months! I was thinking it was more like *a* month. He had been doing some long and hard thinking about proposing to Heather, and finally decided he was ready. I always had a feeling the two would end up together, and now, it's really happening.

What I Didn't See Before

Heather's face turned a blushing red as she slowly walked to the front of the room. Donald kept his eyes on her, as if it was their wedding day and she was walking down the aisle.

"What's going on?" Heather squinted her eyes and laughed. The whole room could sense her anxiety.

"Heather Rose Lumbach," Donald started. "I knew I was in love with you from the first day I met you. I remember the day. It was April 30th, 2002. You were just a shy girl with a big personality waiting to come out."

"My first day of work… you remembered the date." Heather was clearly flattered that he remembered.

"You had your hair curled with a little braid running across the side of your head and you wore scrubs. I just remember thinking 'Wow, she's beautiful.' Then I got to know you and I found you even more beautiful. More than beautiful. I don't think there is a word to describe how I feel about you."

Luca looked back at me, smiled, grabbed my hand, and turned back around to face them. My heart jumped up a little bit. I've never held hands with Luca and it's incredible how my hand fits into his so perfectly. It feels comfortable and delicate.

What I Didn't See Before

"I want to spend my life with you," Donald continued. "I want to raise a family and take your kids in as my own children. I want to spend every moment I can with you and make life a crazy adventure. I want to be the man you come home to every night and wake up with every morning. I want a marriage."

Heather was blushing even harder and her cheeks were twitching from smiling so hard. I could see tiny tears rolling down her face and plopping onto the floor.

Donald stepped down to the floor on one knee and reached into his pocket. He pulled out a ring and looked up to meet Heather's gaze, who was staring at the ring with wide eyes. "Heather, will you do me the honor and be my wife?"

Heather clasped her hands over her mouth, bent over and sobbed. She looked back up at Donald and said through tears, "Yes, yes, absolutely yes!"

Donald and Heather then kissed as the kids cheered for the two. We all clapped and screamed for them, gave each other hugs and some of us even started crying. It was such a sentimental moment to experience. My eyes were stinging from trying to hold back my tears, but nothing was coming out because of how dehydrated I am.

What I Didn't See Before

It was the most magical thing to experience- two people coming together as one. The two of them are absolutely perfect for one another. I only hope one day I will be in love as strong as the two of them are.

Luca raised his water bottle up to the ceiling and crunched it to get everyone's attention.

"Excuse me, excuse me everybody," Luca interjected. "I'd like to raise our water bottles as a toast to these two lovebirds finding true love. Congratulations, and I can safely speak for everyone when I say we wish you all of the best together. Last but not least, you better make me your best man or there will be a serious problem between us."

Donald laughed and Luca waved his hand to signal he was only joking.

"To love!" Luca said. Everyone repeated in unison, "To love!" and we all clashed our water bottles together and celebrated.

"That was quite a night wasn't it?" Luca said as we walked alone together down the long hallways. It was great to see Luca on his feet again after all the work he did in therapy.

"Yeah. It's something I'll remember forever."

"Me too. I teased Heather about a month ago about the two being a couple and she totally denied it. I could sense the lies."

"I know, me too. It was pretty obvious something was going on between them. I wonder why they hid it from us."

"I don't know, maybe because they didn't want to get us all excited until they knew whether it was going to work out between them."

"Yeah, but I can't see it not working out. They were made for each other, you know?"

"Just like mac and cheese and ketchup were made for each other." Luca nodded with his eyebrows raised at me. I scoffed at him, disgusted. "If you'd just give it a chance you'd probably really like it," he said.

"Ketchup and mac and cheese? No thanks, I'm good."

"Well, I'm making food for our dinner date tonight. I'm not saying it's going to be mac and cheese and ketchup, but there's a chance it might be."

I looked at him and stopped walking abruptly. "If you make me that for dinner, I'm not coming."

"We'll just see about that." Luca wiped off his shoulder, trying to be suave and backed up into his room. I rolled my eyes at him and waved goodbye. "I'll be there at 8:15, be ready!"

One thing you don't expect to happen while you're at a hospital is getting asked to go on a date. So in my case, I don't have anything super fancy to put on. Thankfully Kristina is obsessed with clothes and has most of her wardrobe here, so she came to the rescue.

"I like that one on you," she said, giving an approving nod. "It brings out your eyes."

"Yeah? I mean it is pretty, but I don't know. The straps are a little loose. If I bend over you can see my whole chest."

"Well don't bend over then." I looked at Kristina and raised an eyebrow and she said, "Okay, fine, we can see what else I have."

"Ooh!" I exclaimed, picking up a light blue faux wrap dress. It was classy, the type of impression I'd want to give. "I'm trying this one on."

"Good choice. That's my lucky dress."

"How so?"

What I Didn't See Before

"Well," Kristina started pacing the room slowly, which told me she was about to tell me a long story. "I bought it about three years ago on a Black Friday shopping spree. I was with my mom and my sister at the mall and we had basically finished up our shopping. But then I saw that dress in the window of a new boutique. I asked the woman behind the counter how much it was and she told me it was free. She said nobody wanted it because there was a little rip on the bottom of it that couldn't be stitched up."

Kristina picked up the dress and showed me the little rip at the bottom. "It's really small, but it's there. The woman told me it had been sitting there for so long that she decided she was going to keep it up one more day and if nobody bought it, she was going to get rid of it. I decided to buy it and right after I did she said, 'May this bring you good luck'. And guess what? It has. The first time I met you and Joey, I was wearing this dress. When I was told that my chemotherapy was working well, I was wearing this dress. And when my sister and her husband delivered their healthy baby girl, I was wearing this dress. But there is a lot more good that's happened while I was wearing it. If you decide to wear it, I hope it'll do the same for you."

What I Didn't See Before

"Wow. Thanks Kristina." I gave her a hug and shuffled my way into the bathroom to try it on. I am a bit of a perfectionist at times, so it's my goal to not let the rip bother me. The dress hugged my body in a very innocent and dainty way, and it was the perfect length. The bow wrapped around the front added a child-like and fun feel to it. It really did feel comfortable, and the color was one of my favorite shades of blue. It reminds me of the spring skies here in Georgia.

I stepped out of the bathroom and walked towards Kristina. She put her hands to her mouth and nodded her head. "It's perfect."

Chapter 15
Luca
July 3, 2019

The word "cancer" is terrifying in and of itself. I'd see a kid out in public in a wheelchair with a bald head, holding a stuffed animal and smiling and I always thought it was something that happened to other people. I never thought it would happen to me. I never thought I would be here, diagnosed with stage two cancer and fighting for my life.

The only hope I could begin to grasp was Jesus. That's something else I never thought would happen. I thought the idea of religion and faith was for other people, not me. My mind was set on the idea that after you die, there's nothing. But here I am, reading my Bible in bed and waiting for the clock to strike 8:15.

My world flipped upside down- actually, more like right side up- the night of June 16th. It's implanted in my brain now- it's something I'll never forget.

It was around midnight. I was lying in bed, tossing and turning, feeling nauseous from my chemotherapy earlier that day. I kept a bucket next to my bed in case I couldn't make it to the bathroom in time if I needed to puke, which I learned was a very smart idea. It's not fun to phone your nurse every hour to tell her she needs to clean you up along with your vomit that's all over the bed. Nothing was helping me fall asleep. I decided to do some searching on my phone for ways to become tired. I tried almost everything on the internet. I did the breathing, I elevated my legs, I did the whole counting sheep thing. But then I saw something interesting. It said to pray. At this point I was willing to try anything, even things such as praying, which I didn't think would work.

I clasped my hands together, closed my eyes, and bowed my head forward. I just started talking, asking for help to fall asleep. I must have fallen asleep during my prayer because I don't remember saying "amen" or anything like that.

Suddenly, I was in a dream. The most vivid, real life experience dream I'd ever had. There were bright lights all around me in every direction and the sound of humming. The humming was tranquil, calming, and inviting. I blindly walked forward in this dream, into the light. I heard a booming voice, both powerful and peaceful.

"You are my son," it said. "I love you."

I fell down on my knees and cried, out of breath and speechless. Although I couldn't see whose voice it was, or what the man looked like, it was clear he was speaking to me. Just then, five angels appeared in front of me. Their faces were glowing- they looked beautiful. They didn't say anything, but they didn't have to. Their presence was humbling and wonderful enough.

I looked up and cried out. "I'm so sorry!"

Right at that moment my lungs felt revived. My body felt calm and absolutely painless. My gaze was fixed on something coming out from the light. I couldn't make out the face, but I saw white robes, the cleanest and most pure white I have ever seen.

"You are forgiven," it said.

What I Didn't See Before

And then I woke up. By that time it was morning. I had slept through the whole night.

That next morning I talked to Heather about my experience when she came in to give me my meds. She started crying, which made me a little uncomfortable because I don't really know what to do when a woman cries, but it made me feel less crazy. She believed me and agreed that there was no way it was anything other than God himself.

I got saved that very day. June 17th, 2019. For me, there was no point in waiting around for any other signs. I was sold that very second.

Last night I read the story of John the Baptist. I promised Paige I'd wait to read it with her, but I was too excited. Jesus literally says there has never been anyone greater than Him, so I needed to hear what He was about. He and I had some similarities, which was interesting. Before all of these weird things started happening to me, I had doubt. My whole heart was filled with the idea that no God would put me and my family through everything we've been through. Then I started to see some silver lining. I never had a good group of people to care for me and listen to me when I'm struggling. Sure, my

What I Didn't See Before

circumstances aren't the best, but basing faith off our circumstances is not how it should work. John the Baptist was in prison and started to doubt if Jesus was really who He said He was. John sent his disciples to ask Him if He was the Messiah or if they should be expecting somebody else. Jesus met John right where he was instead of condemning him. That's what Jesus does with us every step of the way in our lives.

Sure, I have cancer. Sure, I can barely eat food or drink anything. Sure my dad hasn't called or stopped by to make sure I'm okay. But that's okay. Paige gave me the first step I needed to get my life together- a leap of faith. I took a chance on God and thought maybe if I tried praying, asking for help and trying to believe He would help me, maybe He would answer me. And he did.

I haven't told Paige about any of this, but I'm thinking tonight is the perfect opportunity. I know she's been curious to know who this new me is and where he came from. I don't know why I didn't tell her earlier, I just thought maybe it would fade away. But it hasn't faded, not even a little bit.

Alaina was the first person I told my story to, besides Heather. She hung up the phone in the middle of my story, which was odd. I tried calling her about ten times afterwards but there was no response. About fifteen minutes later she was knocking at my door. She gave me the biggest hug- I honestly think she may have broken my rib cage- and asked me to tell the story over and over again. I couldn't understand why the last time I saw Alaina she stormed out on me the way she did. Now I see why. She just wanted me to have this unexplainable joy- she just wanted the best for me.

    My Mom has been supportive through this entire process. Even though it's not her responsibility necessarily, she's still been coming here and taking care of me. I wonder what my real Mom would think of all of this. It would be a lot easier if she were still here, but I'm thankful to have the friends and family I do right now.

    The clock is inching closer and closer to 8:15. Joey and Kristina offered to help set up a whole dinner scene with a table for two back in one of the empty conference rooms. Kristina went way overboard, setting up streamers and colorful lights all over. I also got them to help me make dinner- mac and cheese with ketchup. I know exactly how she's going to react to that though, so I have a backup of a

What I Didn't See Before

peanut butter and jelly sandwich. It's not the most gourmet meal, but it's all I could put together.

Joey suddenly came barging into my room holding a huge plastic wrapped bag.

I raised an eyebrow of caution and laughed. "Did you kill someone?"

Joey hit the bag against the wall which made hardly any noise, and nodded. "It's go time."

My heart began to race walking up to her door. Not just because walking has been a hard adjustment after being in a wheelchair for so long, but because I really don't want to mess this up. I adjusted the tie Joey let me borrow, knocked on her door softly, and stepped back. The door quickly swung open, and Paige was in a beautiful blue dress. She had a little bit of mascara on, which accentuated her captivating dark brown eyes. Her long brown hair was cascading down her shoulders almost, but not quite, reaching her hips. I couldn't help but look at her. She's just so naturally beautiful.

"What?" Paige giggled.

"Sorry. You look really," I cleared my throat, and let out a small nervous laugh. "You look really beautiful."

"Yeah?" Paige tucked her hair behind her ear which revealed silver studded earrings.

"Yeah."

"Thank you. Same to you."

"I look beautiful?" I said sarcastically, pretending to be insulted.

Paige laughed and hit me in the arm gently. "I meant handsome, silly goose."

"Well thank you, madam," I said, offering my arm for her to wrap hers around. "Shall we?"

Paige linked her arm into mine. "We shall."

We walked off together, arm in arm, smiling harder than I've ever smiled before because I get to spend the evening with *her*. Paige Averi Labelle, the most incredible woman in the universe. The one who's taught me what it's like to be vulnerable and real. It's a life I could get used to.

Somehow I got her to try the mac and cheese with ketchup. It was a tough battle to get her to at least try a bite, but she eventually gave in. I think she actually may have enjoyed it for a second, but about five seconds later she spit it out.

What I Didn't See Before

"Oh, ew!" Paige wiped her mouth and took a swig of her lemonade.

"Are you serious? You don't like it?"

"That may be one of the worst things I've ever tasted."

"Hey, you can't deny there was a split second where you actually seemed to like it."

"Okay," Paige laughed. "A split second. That was before I tasted the horrible combination of cheese and ketchup."

"You don't like cheese or ketchup?"

"No, those are my least favorite foods in the world."

"You're kidding! What do you dip your fries in?"

"Vanilla ice cream."

I gave her a look of disgust and shook my head. "Oh geez. Don't tell me you're one of those people who puts pineapple on your pizza." Paige sunk into her seat, smiled slyly, and slurped on her lemonade through her straw. I sighed, disappointed at this. "No..."

"Oh come on! Have you ever tried it?"

"No! Why would anybody want to do that to themselves?"

"Because it's good!"

"Yeah, no thanks. I don't want any tropical fruit on my savory Italian dish."

Paige shook her head and shrugged. "Don't knock it till you try it."

"Maybe on our one hundredth date you can convince me to do that."

Paige's cheeks slowly turned red. "You think we'll go on a hundredth date?"

"Don't you?" I said, leaning forward, feeling my throat burn as I tried to take a sip of lemonade.

"Yeah, yeah I think so."

Those words comforted me more than any other thing she could've said in that moment. I've never been good at communicating with girls. I always think they're going to shoot me down if I try to have the slightest bit of confidence. But with Paige, it's different. A part of her agrees with my confident and vulnerable side, which gives me hope that maybe one day our relationship will go past hospital dates in empty conference rooms. One day we will be out of here, healthy and happy, in a home of our own.

As the night went on, Paige and I had some of the best conversations I've ever had. It's so easy with her- it

What I Didn't See Before

feels right. She opened up to me about her family and everything going on with her dad. If I were in her shoes, I'd have a hard time as well. If my dad showed up at this hospital one day out of nowhere I'm not sure what I'd do. So for her dad to come back into her life after leaving, I can't imagine how that must feel.

I decided before the night was over to tell her about my dream. I told her about the light, the angels, the voice, and how I felt painless.

"Are you serious?" Paige covered her mouth with her hands.

"I am. It was the most surreal thing that could've ever happened to me. I mean, God actually stepped in and rescued me. He actually saved me, I don't even deserve it, but He cares for me, you know?"

Paige looked me straight in the eyes. Her eyes were full of bewilderment and exposed the deepest parts of herself.

"I think I might be the most happy human alive right now," she said. "I'm so happy you got to experience that. Did you see Him?"

"No, not really. I saw glowing white robes, but the light was so bright that I couldn't make out a face. But I did see one thing that let me know who I was speaking to."

"What?" Paige eagerly asked.

"Red dots in the center of His palms."

Paige's tears began running down her cheek, faster than a river flows. She held up a hand to gesture that she was sorry for crying.

"Don't say it, don't be sorry. I had this exact same reaction when I woke up the next morning," I felt the need to go over there and hold her in my arms as she cried, so she felt less alone. I followed the instinct and scooted my chair over to hers, letting out a small laugh to let her know it was okay. "Come here." She leaned into my chest as I wrapped my arms around her. Everything about this moment is perfect. Holding her, I never wanted to let go.

More than anything I wanted to kiss her, but the new me resisted it until she leaned in. It was quick, gentle, and filled with sentiment. It felt right. My first kiss with the most perfect woman.

What I Didn't See Before

Chapter 16
Paige
July 4, 2019

I stormed into Kristina's room, waking her up from her nap. Fred crashed against the wall which tugged at my port, but I didn't care.

"Paige, I was sleeping."

"I had my first kiss last night!"

Those seven words jolted Kristina out of bed. "You what?" she exclaimed, excitedly.

"I know! I can't believe it either!"

"What! Okay, I'll make the coffee. You, sit down and fix your port. Tell me everything."

The skin around my port has started to look a bit swollen and red. It might even be infected, but my head has been in so many places that this possible infection is the last thing on my mind. I wiped it down with sanitizing wipes and felt my skin ache and burn, screaming at me to do something about it. I ignored it and carried on with my conversation.

"I don't even know where to start. Luca has just been surprising me so much lately. Everything about his demeanor and perspective on life has just taken a sharp right turn. I didn't know what was going on, but then he told me everything."

Kristina and I talked for an hour about Luca, God, family, and our health. I tried to explain to her about my dad, but the words just wouldn't come out. Ever since I had that conversation with my mom, we never mentioned the topic again. I haven't heard from him or seen him at all and I really don't want to. I know forgiveness is important and blah blah blah, but it's hard. Most people don't realize what this feels like. Forgiveness is easier said than done.

Today is the Fourth of July, which means my mom and brother are coming to visit. For the past couple of years they've prepared a huge barbecue for the students here and set up an area on the rooftop deck to watch the fireworks. It's something every one of us looks forward to each year

What I Didn't See Before

because well, there's not much else to get excited about over here. But now I don't know if I'm excited or nervous. The last thing I want is to talk to my mom and brother about my dad.

"Paige!" Joey shouted from down the hallway. I jumped and dropped all of the supplies I was carrying, feeling them hit my chest and slide down it.

"Joey," I said anxiously, ducking down to pick everything up. "You scared me."

"Sorry," Joey rushed to my side and helped me. "I just was going to ask if you needed any help."

"Yeah, thanks. I need to get this stuff up to the deck. Could you-" I couldn't finish my sentence, the pain was intense. I pulled back my shirt and looked down at my port which was a screeching red boiling fleshy disaster.

"Paige," Joey pulled back and looked around to see if any nurses were nearby. "That looks horrible. You need to get that checked out right now before it gets worse."

"No." I countered, hoping he would just drop it.

"What do you mean *no*? That's the worst I've seen a port infection before."

"It's not that bad." Joey looked at me like I was crazy. "What? It's fine, seriously."

What I Didn't See Before

"Paige it won't take long to fix-"

"I said, no." Joey's facial expression completely changed at the sharp tone of my voice. I knew he could sense the sensitive hidden layer underneath my exasperation. I can persist as much as I want with him, and he always finds a way to make me cave, but this time I just won't. "I'm going to do anything I can to see my brother today. I miss him."

Joey nodded in agreement, silencing his every tendency and urge to tell the nurses.

"I'll go get Luca to help set up." Joey patted me on the back, and walked off.

The rooftop deck looked like a mystical garden. The fairy lights enclosed the space with radiant positivity and the evergreen accents made it all the more comforting. It looked as if a wedding could be performed here, so beautiful and elegant. Luca and I sat together by the fire, roasting marshmallows in the sunlight until night drew nearer. He sat me down on the bench, plucked the most vibrant flower from the rooftop garden and tucked it behind my ear. We spun the record player and danced to Beatles songs, laughing and singing, and for the first time in

What I Didn't See Before

forever- I finally felt free. It felt as if my disposition was receiving a makeover- a new flower blossoming in the field of my empty imagination. Every thought in my head vanished. There is no pain, no worrying, and no suffering when we're together. Everything falls into line, like all of the stars in the sky. We are a rarity. We are Jupiter and Saturn aligning, creating a heavenly masterpiece.

It wasn't long before all this enchanting melody of an evening was put to a halt. I can't imagine what my face looked like right then, what lasted for a flicker of a moment in my eyes would change the pace of tomorrow. *He* was standing in the doorway. *He- my dad.* His face was ruggedly handsome and his eyes were observant of the rooftop, but mostly of me. I could hear Luca whispering gently behind me that everything was going to be fine and that this is just something that needs to happen. That I need to forgive him, that I need to at least speak a few words to him. It felt as if the music faded completely away and all I could hear was the ringing inside my ears, the gentle whisper of Luca, and the voices in my head giving me every reason not to talk to this man. My head is entangled with this dilemma of what to do next and it's getting much harder to silence the instinct to just run away and hide from this. But then again, I run from everything that matters. I run from things that get in the way of the grudges I pay daily to keep.

  So, I felt my body move forward, closer and closer to him. My feet were moving as if they were unconscious, as if this was muscle memory, as if this is the last they remembered doing when I previously saw my dad. His smile was sunken in and I could sense his arms were ready to be opened wide. The voices faded away little by little, until all that was left were Luca's whispers. Although I may have no sensitivity towards this man, I can spot my brother out of the corner of my eye. His eyes are glimmering. He wants this green light of absolution as much as he and my mom.

  "Hi," I managed to get out, feeling the heat of erythema rush over my skin. He didn't seem confident with me standing in front of him which honestly made me feel a lot less anxious. I felt like I had at least a grain of power in his presence, but I was still unsure of what to say..

  "It's hard to believe I actually have the opportunity to see you again," he said. "I know that I don't deserve it, and you don't owe me anything."

"I know I don't," I stammered in between my words and looked up to my mom and brother. "But I don't see why we can't start over."

My dad's face lit up, his dimples formed and his perfectly straight teeth grinned at me. I could see a little tear form in the corner of his right eye- a happy tear.

"Oh," my dad wrapped his arms around me and I could feel his heart beating vibrantly on my chest. He pulled away and looked at me in the eyes. "You mean it?"

"Yeah, I do."

He hugged me again, and my brother Brayden began to clap his hands together and cheer which then had everyone else joining in.

"You!" I cried, throwing my arms around my brother. "I missed you!"

"I missed you so much, G!" Brayden exclaimed as he nuzzled up in my arms.

My mom was holding my dad's hand, crying against his shoulder. "Paige," she said, letting go of his hand and joining mine. "You giving your dad a second chance is the most wonderful thing that has ever happened to me. Thank you so much honey."

What I Didn't See Before

"We've had some long conversations about this decision," my dad jumped in. "I should have never left. I thought it was the right decision. I tried searching for something to fill the gap in my life but after leaving I only made it more empty. I've realized now that the gap missing was a real and authentic relationship with God. After I found Him he led me right back to this family. Everything feels complete now and I will do anything to prove that to you because I love you."

I swallowed my pride as the voices in my head came again trying to bring the grudge back to life.

"You don't have to say it back. I know it's going to take time and it doesn't offend me. I take full responsibility for this situation that I put you, your brother, and your mom in. And I know that it's never going to be the same."

This whole situation played out totally different in my head. I wanted to hurt him, spite him, say anything to make him realize how much pain he'd caused me. I wanated to make him realize that I've gone through years of therapy trying to get help, but have gotten nowhere because of him. But at this moment I can't do any of that. Seeing him again with this new perspective of family, God, and life softened my heart. All I want to do is tell him that I love him and I missed him so much. To tell him that I missed us throwing the baseball in the backyard, baking cookies late at night in the kitchen because neither of us could sleep, and climbing the tallest trees then freezing up because we were both too afraid to climb back down. I just want my dad back.

"Dad," I say quietly, clearing my throat. "I really wanted to be mad at you. But I just can't. I've missed you."

"I've missed you more than anything."

My life felt as if three thousand tons of weight were plucked off of it. My heart felt as if it grew three thousand times bigger, and the voices in my head grew three thousand times quieter. My life needed this very thing, even if I couldn't see the full picture. I can already imagine how tomorrow will go. Dr. Woods will ask if I've thought about forgiving my dad and I'll tell her I saw him again and forgave him. She'll be in the best, brightest and bushy-tailed mood anyone has ever seen, and Heather will shower me in hundreds of hugs. I can finally move on to new and better things with a full family again, not just pieces of one. Sure, things will never be the same as they were before, but maybe they'll be better.

What I Didn't See Before

Never in the years of picturing this moment did this scenario run through my head. I guess there are some things you really can't see before they happen.

What I Didn't See Before

Chapter 17
Luca
July 6th 2019

Every day it has been getting harder to breathe. My lungs feel as if they're filled with tar and the air is trapped underneath it, trying desperately to break free. The coughs are as good as nothing. Anytime something even as small as a drop of water hits my throat, it ignites. My ribs are now completely visible and my arms can barely lift anything heavier than five pounds. But on the bright side, things could be much worse. I have the most incredible girlfriend and the most wonderful group of friends.

That's right. Paige and I made it official. I was hoping the story would be a little more romantic, but how was I supposed to know that acid reflux was going to crash the party? It was an amazing day though, nonetheless, and that's all that matters.

Her dad plans on coming a couple times a week to check up and spend time with her. I kind of wanted to hate him for everything he did to Paige, but he really is impossible to hate. He has this joy about him that's more contagious than a cold. Plus, this whole overwhelming new perspective on life makes it difficult to be too negative.

Thanks to her, I've realized that journaling is the perfect outlet to any stress. It used to be running but, you know, cancer, legs growing weaker. I know journaling isn't the most "manly" thing you could do for a hobby, but I've learned that sensitivity is way more important than being all macho. That comment could make any players out there scoff- I know that for a fact because I used to be one. It's a game changer when you start to actually admire the character of someone, not their appearance.

"Kid," Heather nudged my shoulder and handed me a cup of water. "Time for your night meds."

I grabbed the cup from her, popped all the pills in my mouth and swallowed them all with one big swig, clenching my fists and gritting my teeth as the burning sensation peeled its way down my throat.

"You're a natural at this point," she said.

"How's Paige holding up?" I asked her, partly to distract myself and partly because I was hoping the answer would be somewhat positive.

"The infection is pretty severe, but you know Paige. She'll be alright."

"Can I see her?"

"Well sure hun', but not tonight, it's too late and you just took three milligrams of Eszopiclone. Not sure you'll stay awake long enough to say so much as two words to her."

"Fair enough. And for the record, if I would've known her infection was that bad I would've told you."

"I know. That was her responsibility, I'm not mad at you so you can relax." She smiled, patted me twice on the back, and headed for the door. "Goodnight kiddo, sleep well alright?"

"Okay," I replied, distracted. "You too."

She raised an eyebrow at me and laughed. "You think I sleep working at a place like this? Ha! That's a good one." She went to close the door but swung it back open, pointing her finger at me. "By the way, I sure as heck won't sleep if you sneak out to her room. Am I clear?"

Her deep Georgia southern accent and the concern in her voice made me realize the seriousness of the situation even through her lightheartedness.

"Got it."

July 7, 2019

My brother Devin and my older sister Lila both promised they'd swing by this evening to keep me company while Paige was recovering. It's been awhile since I've seen the two of them since they both went off to college. Even though the two of them are twins, I've never seen two people more different from each other. Devin is this put together man who knows exactly what he wants and is more sophisticated than my own dad, while Lila is this wild and mysterious gothic girl who barely speaks. The past me thought of her as my role model. I always wanted to do as much as she did, go out to tons of parties, meet total strangers and not come back home for weeks. That's exactly how she's been living her life for almost three years now and I can't help but wonder if she actually likes that whole scene. I don't think I could ever do that now. Life has a lot more meaning to it.

What I Didn't See Before

  I think of it like this, in the simplest way possible. When I grow up and have kids, what kind of father should I be to them? What kind of father would they need the most? *That's* the person I want to become. I want to become a real man, not a childish boy who will have to get his act together last second.

  These kinds of thoughts flood my mind often now. I don't ever think about the things I used to spend days daydreaming about. I know there'll be moments of weakness to come but my head is currently above the water and I plan on keeping it there.

  "How are you feeling?" I shoot over to Paige on my phone, knowing she probably is still sleeping but crossing my fingers she isn't. I worry about her. She's so headstrong and puts every human before herself. I picture that if she weren't sick right now, she'd be helping the kids down in the Pediatric Intensive Care Unit, coloring pictures of Elmo and laughing with them. *That's* the kind of person she is. A godly, young, intelligent, motherly figure. I know for a fact that she will make an amazing mother one day.

  Donald appointed me one of the groomsmen, Joey also, so he came by to drop off the suits. "This one is yours, should fit alright."

What I Didn't See Before

"These are sharp. Don't know the last time I actually wore one of these things."

"Me either. They're so itchy." He laughed and sat down on the edge of my bed, checking his watch. "Don't you have to be somewhere in a little?"

"What? Oh, yeah. Occupational Therapy. It's fine, I should get there in time." I flipped over my phone, which to no surprise, there was no text from Paige.

"Something on your mind?"

"Just worried about Paige."

"Yeah." He scooted a little closer to me and sniffled. "We all are. The staph infection has yet to clear up. It's gone down a little though if that helps at all."

"Eh. Has her fever gone down?"

"A little bit. I was down there a bit ago, she seems to be holding up alright." Donald opened his mouth to say something else but then shut it and looked down.

"What?"

"Promise me you won't get too worried."

"Okay," I responded uneasily.

"She was diagnosed with Sepsis late last night."

What I Didn't See Before

"*Sepsis?* Are you serious? She's not going to go into Septic Shock is she? How serious is it? Is she on antibiotics? How bad is it?"

"It's hard to tell," he said, scratching his head. "We're doing all we can for her but she let the infection go on so long it unfortunately got worse. She has a whole team of doctors making sure she's stable at all times."

My heart was beating uncontrollably, and I could feel sweat forming all over my body. *Sepsis?* Donald might as well have told me she got the death sentence. That's *exactly* what Sepsis is for a cancer patient, especially one like her.

"Can I still see her?" I asked desperately.

"You can, it's not contagious. But I wouldn't go for long. She's not really up for lots of company." Donald frowned and put his hand on my shoulder. "I know this isn't something you wanted to hear and I would excuse you from OT but I think you need to go. It'll be good to see everyone and get your mind off of things."

"Yeah, okay." I scratched my neck and got up to get dressed as Donald left my room. I would talk to Joey about this but I don't think he even knows which makes it twenty times harder because I can't even discuss this with anyone.

What I Didn't See Before

But on the other hand, I wouldn't want to scare anyone and put them in the state of mind I'm currently in.

The walk to OT felt long. My legs felt like they were going to give out beneath me, so it felt good to sit down. Everyone around me was their cheerful positive self, talking to each other and laughing. I felt out of place, unable to shake the thought of Paige suffering and alone. It's not fair that she's sitting in a dark and cold room.

A hand pounded against my back. "What's up," Joey smiled and slumped down into the seat next to me. His face looked sunken in, as if he'd been crying all morning.

"Hey," I said with a curious tone. "You okay?"

"Oh yeah, I'm fine."

"You sure?"

"Yes, I'm fine," He looked at the clock on the wall, to the door, and back to the clock. "Just really tired. I didn't sleep much last night."

That's when it hit me. Donald probably had dropped off his tux too and told him about Paige.

"It's gonna be okay," I said, my tone completely unsure of itself.

"Yeah." He rubbed the back of his neck, breathing deeply as he pulled his hand away.

What I Didn't See Before

Dr. Woods walked into the room, dragging an easel behind her. She looked uneasy but relaxed, uncomfortable but present. She was best at hiding her emotions. After all, she studies them. She knows how to manipulate them and use them in moments like these.

Paige's news will soon be spreading throughout the whole building of Saint Andrews, everyone will be affected. Sepsis, the death sentence. I want to ask what the doctors think of it. I want to ask if they believe she's going to make it out alive. Joey's mind is all over the wall, scattered and unorganized, but all fixated on one thought. Kristina's having too much fun laughing with Audrey and Clara to know about any of it.

"Hey," I nudged Joey. "Think we can sneak out of here?"

"What?"

"We should go see her."

Joey's face deepened in thought, as if he was having a flashback. He nodded his head, smiled, and nudged me back. "Let's do it. She'd do the same for any of us."

Joey and I ducked through the hallways of the psych wing, trying to avoid any nurse or doctor in sight. It was becoming a little game, like we were diehard fans trying to get past security to attend a concert. Oddly enough, it took my mind off of everything going on and reminded me it's okay to live in the moment and not worry too much about the what if's or what's going to happen in the next five minutes.

That was, until we reached Paige's room. I took a deep breath, closed my eyes, bowed my head, and prayed through my imagination. The words weren't coming from my mouth but they were more powerful than ever in my head, bouncing from one request to another. I've never seen one with my eyes, but miracles do happen. They still exist and anyone who believes there's room for one to take place will have healed faith and a new perspective on life. Paige has that perspective. *I* have that perspective. *Paige isn't going to die, she's going to be okay.* She's the reason I am who I am now. She's the reason I ever explored any depth in my faith whatsoever. She's the reason this life changing disease feels a lot less lonely. She's the reason my mind is sound. She's the reason I haven't escaped what should be a hell hole of a place but is now my saving grace.

My life changed because of her. If I were alone in my hospital room, diagnosed with alcoholic gastritis alone,

What I Didn't See Before

I would still be the same. If I were alone going through my first rounds of chemotherapy of esophageal cancer, I would still be the same. It's not the diseases that complement you, it's the people who love you. It's not the diseases that define you, it's God that defines you. It's not the diseases that make you unique, it's the purpose and story you'll have to share one day.

Paige made me realize there's more to life than a party. Life is more than one big celebration and blur. It's a radiant mural decorated with each and every memory, the good and the bad. And now, at seventeen years old, her mural is one seventh of the way finished, but could be done. This could be it. Her mural deserves to be finished.

I knocked at the door cautiously, hoping for a voice of tranquility and gentleness to ring "Come in!" but it never happened. I opened the door, Joey behind me, and we walked in together.

Her face was pale and discolored. Her eyes were closed. Her body was twitching, shivering, quaking. Her head was bare, and her eyebrows almost invisible. The machines hooked up to her were taking up more than half of the room. I could hear my heart beating, and my face flushing- my heart dropping.

What I Didn't See Before

The strongest young woman I know, in complete surrender. Everything is up to God now. Her fate lies in His hands. His miraculous, life-healing, deaf-hearing, blind-seeing, dumb-speaking, paralyzed-leaping hands.

I crouched down next to her, grabbing her cold yet sweaty hand in mine. A tear rolled down my cheek and plopped onto my hand, sinking between my fingers and falling into her palm. Her face was still, mouth closed. I could feel her pulse and see her stomach rise and fall, rise and fall, until both our breathing rates were the same. I wanted more than anything to talk to her, to comfort her and tell her I'm here for her. But for now, this will do.

"Is her pulse normal?" Joey's face was pale as white silk.

"Yes," I said, looking back at her. "It feels good."

He slumped down on the other side of her, grabbing her other hand in his. "It's so cold," he weeped. "I've never seen her like this before."

"She's going to make it through."

"I think so too." Joey cracked a smile, but his smile didn't last long. He buried his face in Paige's arm and began to cry silently.

What I Didn't See Before

My head wandered back and forth from "God, why aren't you doing something?" to, "God, I know you will do something." It's hard, this whole faith thing. Hope and faith seem like comforting words, but both are way easier said than done. What's happening to Paige is something I never want to see again, and hope I won't. I don't know what the outcome of this will be, but I have to try and have faith that she'll make it through.

But just then her pulse couldn't be felt anymore.

What I Didn't See Before

Chapter 18
Paige
July 7 2019

Two seals were tossing back and forth in the water as the waves toppled over them, crashing back and forth onto the shore. A boat was headed to shore and the coast had never looked this pretty. As if misplaced, two penguins came waddling towards me.

"You are supposed to be in the Arctic," I said.

They waddled closer, and I laughed at the two of them. Two penguins on a beach. You don't see that every day. I picked up my light brown woven bag and swung it over my shoulder. The walk to the house wasn't long from the shore, about a mile. Palm trees danced in the wind, the feeling of an incandescent wind swept over my salt watered

What I Didn't See Before

body, warming me up in an instant. Quick as it was wet, my hair was dry.

I looked back to see the penguins waddling behind me, following me back to the house. Bright, optical lights from the cave flashed in front of my eyes and drew me near. Rolling over the stone I found it full of animals. Polar bears, arctic foxes, snowy owls, harp seals, snowshoe rabbits, and more. Each and every one of them was still, waiting for me to speak.

"You are supposed to be in the Arctic," I said. They stared at me, some cocking their heads and some widening their eyes. "You shouldn't be here."

I left the stone open, walking back to my house. The curious animals followed behind me. The shack door was left ajar, which was strange. I shut it on the way out, I thought.

I walked into a house full of ice, snow, and freezing waters. The kitchen was nowhere to be seen, both the couches and the bed gone. Everything was covered. The animals followed me in, back to a more appropriate habitat. They jumped into the polar waters, rolled in the snow, and began to relax into their environment.

What I Didn't See Before

"There, this is where you belong now," I said to them.

A voice thundered, shaking the house.

"Paige, you belong in a land more beautiful and enchanting than this, but everything comes in time. For now, you belong back with your family. Be free, and be healed."

I gasped for air, sitting up straight. My eyes rolled back into place. My heart was beating frantically. There I was, in a room full of doctors. Lights blinding me, machines suffocating me. My head was light and my body was painless. I felt like a feather, light and airy. Everything about this moment was different. The look on everyone's faces when they saw me was full of bewilderment. They were astonished, but why?

But then, I saw him. The very person I wanted to see.

"Paige?" Luca said, his face looked sickly and dumbfounded.

I smiled at him and he ran at me, plowing through everyone else in the room. I wrapped my arms around him and rested my head on his shoulder. I could feel his body's little tremors as his tears hit my shoulder.

What I Didn't See Before

"I thought you were gone."

"You can't get rid of me that easily," I said, noticing that I was also crying, trying to hold back everything that just happened. He apologized for crying, but I embraced this moment because he's not someone who strikes me as a crier.

"Paige," Joey ran to me and Luca backed away for him. He hugged me and talked through tears. I pretended to be flattered but I really had no idea what he was saying, it was all a bunch of gibberish.

After an hour of talking to my friends, Dr. Huffman walked in with the team of nurses and her mouth opened agape.

"Honey," she started on. "I don't know how this happened. You were brain dead and flatlined for four minutes. Now your sepsis is completely cleared."

"What?" I questioned in astonishment.

"It's gone. We checked and ran all the tests. And your cancer, well, it's gone now, Paige."

My breath felt like it was completely sucked back into my body, making it impossible for me to get the words out.

"It's, it's gone? After four year it's all of a sudden gone?"

I could see Heather squeezing Donald's hand, both of them near tears; exhausted. She smiled at me, blithesome.

"You're cured."

The words rang through my head and I felt them sweep over me, completely melting me and forming me into a new golden masterpiece. My heart leaped out of my chest and up to the heavens in bewilderment and all the while knowing this was a miracle. God saved me. God had saved Luca, and now God had saved me. We may be saved in completely different ways, but we are often saved in ways we never expected.

Luca probably never expected to be diagnosed with cancer, lying in a hospital bed most of the day trying to roll to the opposite side of his bed without throwing up. He probably never expected before to see and hear the voice of God.

Just as I didn't expect to experience those things. *I got to hear the voice of God.* I never expected to make it out of here alive. I always had the expectation that cancer

What I Didn't See Before

was going to be the death of me. I never thought I'd be cured.

The room was filled with cheer, happiness, and exhilaration. Luca's hand was in mine, squeezing it tighter than ever and shaking it around. Joey's head was laid against my shoulder, sobbing as the tears absorbed into my t-shirt material. I couldn't feel any pain, my body felt light and new. The room didn't feel as claustrophobic as it usually does. It felt like I could finally breathe. I couldn't explain how deep the goodness of God was, especially in this moment. It's indescribable. He lifted me from the depths of death, rescued me, and called me by name. Now, I have full hope that Luca will survive this too.

July 9 2019

The dinner party was incredible. The chefs at the hospital went full out for me, making my favorite meals; pot roast, garlic mashed potatoes, honey glazed carrots, and a decadent chocolate cake with buttercream frosting.

My mom, dad, and brother all showed up for the occasion in their fanciest clothes and bought me a dress of my own to change into. They were all in tears at the news of me being clear of cancer and that I could finally come home, although, there is a part of me that doesn't want to leave this building. Saint Andrews has been a part of me for a long time and the thought of leaving to go home is bittersweet.

My plan is to start learning to drive as soon as possible so I can get my license and come here and visit whenever I can. Heather signed me up for driving school some time ago while I was here, so I completed everything I could online, so I had a jump start to get my license.

"Hey, Luca," I walked up behind him and put my hand on his shoulder. "How are you?"

He turned around to face me with the biggest smile on his face. "I couldn't be happier, I've been praying about this every night."

"You have?"

"Yeah, and listen. I know I have to stay here but we're going to be fine. It's way more important to me that you're healthy than anything else. On days you can't be here, we can video chat. We can figure out anything that works for us to be able to talk. And trust me, as soon as I get out of here the first place I'll be going is to see you."

What I Didn't See Before

I grabbed both of his hands, pushed up on my tippy toes, and planted a kiss on his cheek. "You're the most wonderful man. I've already made a deal with my parents to stay here three days out of the week. The staff is allowing me to stay in the guest sleeping area. I'm not going to leave you, Luca. I want to be here for all your treatments and by your side during the hard moments and the happy ones. I'm not going anywhere."

He put his arms around me and pulled me in. I could feel his rib cage against my stomach, and his frail touch around my back. I knew he was growing weaker day by day, but I still have every ounce of hope he will make it out of here. "I love you," he whispered.

Those words are powerful. Every part of my brain was telling me not to say it back, but this little voice inside of me said it was okay. That God is love. That if I feel like this man really could be my husband one day, it was okay. "I love you too."

What I Didn't See Before

Chapter 19

Luca

July 14 2019

Just like that, she was out of here. I stood in the door of her old hospital room trying to pull myself together. I'm beyond happy that she's cured and now can live a full life, but I miss her. I miss being able to walk down the hall and see her nuzzled up in her reading corner with a good book. I miss walking into the cafeteria and watching her fling grapes at the nurses. I miss hearing her sing while she is cleaning, humming away to a song she made up on the spot.

    When Devin and Lila came to visit I couldn't stop mentioning her to them. They laughed at me, making fun of how smitten I was. I don't expect her to drop everything and come see me. She's going to have a new life, free of illness. I just hope she doesn't forget about me because I see her in everything.

I see her when I think about the future. I never would've imagined in my lifetime that I'd want to have children, but when I think of raising them with her, I want a million of them. I want to raise them to fear God and love Jesus. To love others and always lift people up. I know this is far into the future, but I see it all with her.

I see her when I think about music. She's every classical and elegant song composed into one piece. Every time I close my eyes, I picture her and how she moves, so graceful and willowy.

I could seriously picture her changing the world someday with her intelligence. She has all of the components of a perfect woman. And now, I can't help but wonder what she wants to do with her life?

I can see her working in a place like this, working to heal the sick, giving them life advice, and becoming each and every one of their friends. I can see her working in a creative field, composing music or writing stories. I can see her as a teacher, giving wisdom to the young. I can see her as an artist, escaping with the stroke of a brush against an empty canvas. I see her in everything.

    The physically empty room stares back at me, pronouncing hundreds of memories of the two of us, like the first time I walked into her room and saw her drawing a flower on the wall. She pulled back quickly, worried it was someone who worked for the hospital and stood up to block it. When she saw it was me, she sighed and stepped back to show me. I walked to the spot on the wall and pulled back the wall decor to find the flower she had drawn. It was effortlessly beautiful, sketched with a mechanical pencil and her delicate touch. The center was purple and the petals were green, everything was uneven, but so originally hers. Her initials were placed underneath it, P.L. Paige Labelle.

    Her name is so fitting; Paige meaning helpful and Labelle meaning beautiful. A beautiful helper she is indeed, always willing to give someone in need an extra hand. And now that she is healthy, she'll be able to help people all over outside this hospital. Georgia is a populated state; she'll never run out of clients.

    Joey and I are pretty much a duo for right now, which is still great. He's become my best friend over these past couple of months and taught me a lot about the importance of the little things, such as this flower here on the wall staring back at me.

I could feel the presence of someone behind me and sure enough, it was Joey. He and I both stared at the flower together in silence. It seemed as if she was dead and we were staring at one of the only things we had left of her. But this wasn't the case at all. She is healthy and happy outside of this hospital with her family somewhere. I realized something- the patterns of the flower were quite intricate. I grabbed Joey's shoulder and led him out of the room.

"Where are we going?" he said, looking around as we simultaneously waved to our friends and the nurses as we passed.

"She left something."

"What?"

"The flower, did you notice how it wasn't really flower shaped?'

"Yeah, but I mean, she always had trouble making things proportional."

"It's the exact shape of this wing in the hospital. I think she was trying to leave a message."

What I Didn't See Before

"Maybe we should call her. I think we both just miss her," Joey said, pulling his phone out of his pocket.

"No." I smacked the phone out of his hand and it hit the ground.

"Hey, you could've broke-"

"I'll pay for it, let's go." I began walking again, knowing exactly where I was heading.

"With what money? It's not like we can really get a job right now."

Joey grabbed his phone and raced to catch up with me.

"The center of the flower, it was purple, but everything else was green. What room is purple?"

"The teen room," Joey exclaimed very unenthusiastically.

"You'll understand what I'm getting at soon, come on."

We walked through the halls and Joey talked my ear off, I was half paying attention to what he was saying because I was too focused on what Paige may have wanted to say. There was something unusual about the center of the flower- a small brown square in the center of it with the initials "CRP" written in faint pencil. I may be way out of line here and it could be a coincidence, but I'm determined to see if there is anything there, even if it's just the slightest bit of information.

As I walked into the room, I froze. My eyes fixed on the very thing, the small brown box I knew she was talking about- the record player. It was placed in the center of the room, open with a record placed inside of it, one that I've never seen before. It was blank. Beside what I knew was already going to be there, was a note from Paige:

Dear Luca,

I knew you'd find this. These next couple of weeks are going to be difficult for both of us, so I left something for you to make it seem like I'm right there with you. Maybe you didn't wonder, or maybe you did wonder what I did every night after I took my sleeping meds. I decided to document my days with you and record them on a voice memo from the beginning to my very last date with you. I can't wait to see you again. Trust me, it will be sooner than you know. Remember, I have a list of all your chemotherapy treatments. I won't be missing any of them.

Love, Paige.

P.S. Joey if you're there with him, I didn't forget about you. I know your schedule too.

"Okay, so you were right. CRP, check record player," Joey said, finally admitting that my wild goose chase was worth something.

"I can't believe she did this. This is by far the best gift I've ever gotten. She's just incredible."

"She is that. She's never had any trouble with being creative, that's for sure. And hey, I may have been skeptical of you and Paige at first, but that's just because she's my best friend. I just want the best for her and I see now that you're it."

Joey swung his hand to meet the middle of my back and I reciprocated. He knew I wasn't much of a hugger, so this was his way of doing it as an alternative. It meant a lot to hear those things from Joey. When I first got here I had a feeling they were fond of each other in a more than friends type of way, but I quickly learned they were just good friends and that was all. He was kind of like her older brother, but now that we're friends I'm on his good side which makes it both easy and difficult. It keeps me in line to treat Paige the way she should be treated, but I know if I

What I Didn't See Before

ever fall out of bounds that his fist is going to meet the middle of my face.

Alaina hasn't been too vocal the past couple weeks, but to be fair, I haven't texted her much. So my plan today was to see if I could in some way see her, even if it was just over video chat for a couple minutes. I called her and it rang a couple times and ended. Then I called her again and it did the same. "Third times a charm" didn't work either, so I decided to put my phone away and read my Bible.

The woman with the blood issue had such an interesting story that really resonated with me. I remember Paige rambling on about this story one of the first times we ever talked but I didn't quite understand what she was getting at. Now, I see. As little as the gesture may have been for her to touch Jesus' robe, it spoke volumes. Her faith healed her.

Paige's faith healed her. Through all of her years battling leukemia, she never lost faith in God. She never doubted that He wasn't there with her. Did she have doubts? Yes, and I know that because we talked about them all the time. But the one thing she held onto was the knowledge she had that Jesus was real.

What I Didn't See Before

"Luca," Joey burst into my room, out of breath and dazed.

I stood up, seeing his face go white as he struggled to get his words out. "They just rushed your sister in. She's hurt."

Chapter 20
Paige
July 15 2019

Life at home was weird. Well, not life itself, but the adjustment. I know deep down this is a great thing for me, but it feels so off. I'm used to a life full of medication and routine, walking up and down the hallways of the hospital. But now I'm just walking up and down these small hardwood floor hallways.

I guess on the bright side it's been great to spend time with my family. My dad has been doing a ton of work around the house, taking the dogs for a walk, and he's always playing outside with my brother. He promised me that once I was up for it he'd like to start practicing pitching with me again. Honestly, it sounds like everything I've ever wanted, minus one certain thing.

I know that this house is where I'm supposed to be, not at a hospital crowded with other sick people, but I just miss my family there. I miss waking up and seeing all of them for breakfast in the teen room. I miss the scent of hand sanitizer that I complained about almost every day. I miss the loud chatter at night when I was trying to sleep so I'd try to drown it out with my *Sleepy Times* playlist. Everything was just comfortable for me. Now I have to get used to this new style of living- how life should be.

"How've you been sleeping?" My mom said, sitting down next to me with a cup of coffee in her hand.

We both sat by the back window watching Dad and Brayden playing soccer in the backyard. It was a nice picture, the family finally back together and happy again.

"A lot better. I got so used to my bed at Saint Andrews that I've forgotten what a real mattress feels like."

My Mom laughed and smiled at me. "You look healthy, Paige. I know it's only been a few days and it's gonna be a work in progress, but, I don't know. You don't look sick anymore."

What I Didn't See Before

"Well good. That better fade completely cause I want my hair back."

"Aw honey, you will and it'll look so beautiful! It'll be new and healthy and that gorgeous light brown color that you got from your father. Thank Heavens you didn't get my hair."

"Oh, stop, your hair is pretty!"

Her hair was a dirty blonde shade with a hint of red in it. It never really made sense to me where the red came from since we don't know anybody in our family who has red hair, but I was always a little envious of her dash of red hair. I wanted a defining characteristic that was different from everyone else whom I shared blood with, and having cancer isn't really what I wanted to base it off of.

"So," my Mom's eyes looked directly into my soul. "Who's the boy?"

Her words caught me off guard and I let out a half laugh, almost embarrassed to have this conversation. "Excuse me?"

"Come on, I'm your mom. I can sense these things." I looked at her, raising an eyebrow. "Plus I saw you guys dancing on the rooftop."

"He's just this really sweet boy who keeps surprising me. Do you remember when I told you that night on the phone that there was this new boy and I felt connected to him in a way I couldn't explain? It feels like there's some kind of underlying purpose of me meeting him. I found out a lot about him and he became this vulnerable, God-fearing boy. It took a bit of time to break him at first, but I was eventually able to."

"So you like him then?" My mom's smirk widened and the sides of her lips went further and further upwards.

"Yes…"

"Did you kiss him?"

Her eyes were now widening with her smile which made me laugh at how ridiculous she looked. She used to do this all of the time with any drama pertaining to boys when I was in middle school. It always made me uncomfortable, so I'd just spill the tea right then and there. I haven't had these little talks with her in so long. Back then, I used to get so annoyed by these conversations and I'd wish more than anything for them to stop. But now, I'm realizing just how much I love my family and how happy I am to be with them again.

"I'm really happy to be home, Mom."

What I Didn't See Before

I smiled at her and she smiled back, grabbing my hand and patting it twice.

"Fine, don't answer my question. You've earned a free pass this time."

"Is there any way I could maybe go visit tonight? Just for a couple of hours."

"Sure honey, I don't mind. I can take you around five o'clock if that seems like a good time for you."

"Five sounds good. Thanks, Mom."

I gallivanted back upstairs to my bedroom searching through my sheets for my phone to text Luca. My room was bright, the walls mostly made up of windows which poured in sunlight from every angle. It was a light pink color filled with accents of gold and greenery. This room is where my new memories will start. Things will change and be different, but in a way that God intended. This new life is for me, and as weird as I feel about change, this is a good change.

Chapter 21
Luca
July 15 2019

"Did he do this to you?" I all but shouted.

Alaina's body was beaten. The side of her head was bashed in, and dried blood covered most of her face. The only human capable of doing this to Alaina is our father. She was always full of so much spirit, to see her in this position was petrifying.

"He's going through something right now-"

"I don't care what he's going through! He hurt you! That's not how a Dad should treat his own flesh and blood, Alaina."

"He lost his job."

What I Didn't See Before

To be quite honest, I wasn't sure how to react to this news. I always had the mindset that he couldn't lose his job since he founded the company. He's been so caught up in his work that he's forgotten all about us. I always had the thought that the only good thing about him is the fact that he could provide for us, and I still kind of believe that until he can prove us otherwise.

"It's not your fault that he lost his job, it's his! They probably fired him because he comes into work hungover every morning. What did he do to you? Is anything broken?"

"No, but I'm pretty sure I have a concussion."

"Did they check? They need to check, I'll get them right now. What did he do to your head?"

"He um, he hit me with a wooden cutting board."

"*He hit you on the head with that?* Alaina, you're lucky you're not dead! I mean seriously, that could've killed you! I swear, next time I see him I'll-"

I fell to the floor, collapsing. My lungs were out of air, my chest was aching, and my cough was intensifying by second.

"Luca," Alaina put her hand on my back. "You're okay, it's okay."

Her voice calmed me and my coughing fit soon subsided.

"I'm sorry. You shouldn't have to be the one worrying about me. I'm sorry I wasn't home to stop this from happening. It's not fair. Devin and Lila have moved away, Mom's gone, now I'm stuck at this hospital and you're there by yourself."

"I have Mom."

"Our step-mom, she's not our real mom."

I could see by the look on her face that the words hurt. She and our step-mom had developed a really close relationship over the years. They're practically best friends, besides her and Anna.

"I'm sorry, I love her just like she's our real mom, I'm just angry. I should've been there protecting you."

"This isn't your fault. You're working on getting better here and that's all I want for you, okay?"

I shook my head, still feeling guilty, but understanding of her point.

"Besides, this is good for dad. He might actually get back to reality and be the man he was before. Our job is to be there for him and treat him with love, just like Jesus does for us every day. Trust me, once and a while it's hard for me to stay quiet. I want to get mad and scream at him. Sometimes I want to run away, but it's not my job to do that. You wanna see Dad in heaven someday, right?"

"I mean, yeah."

"Then we've got to be the ones to help inspire the change."

A couple months ago these would have been nothing but empty words. It's not easy to bite your tongue, especially when it comes to family. But Alaina was right, we've got to be the ones to help him. None of us have ever tried to seek him out first or try to spend time with him. When I get back home, my number one goal is to try to catch him right after work and just have a conversation with him. I don't know the last time I actually had a real talk with him. He must be extremely lonely knowing his kids don't ever try to bother with him, but it's not like he makes it easy.

"Deal. But after they treat you, could I just see if you could stay here in one of the guest rooms? I just don't like the idea of you going home yet. Plus, it would be nice to spend some time with you."

"That would be nice."

What I Didn't See Before

Paige had shot me a text that she was planning on coming by tonight. I was ecstatic knowing she wanted to come back and see me even though her life at home is probably so much better than her life here. It excites me knowing that one day we won't have to worry about her coming here anymore. I know that I'm not cancer free yet, and my symptoms certainly haven't gone down, but there's hope for me.

She burst through my hospital room doors with the brightest smile stretching across her golden skin. It hasn't been long since I've seen her but it feels like I've been waiting years for this moment.

"Hey you," she said after giving me a warm hug. "How're you holding up?"

"I'm okay actually. Alaina's here."

"She is? That's nice of her to visit, I'll have to say hello-"

"No, that's not the reason."

Her smile faded and her eyebrows furrowed inwards.

"It's my dad's fault."

"Did he-"

"Yes." I knew exactly what she was going to ask.

What I Didn't See Before

"He *can* get better. He's my dad and he deserves a better life. Alaina said he got fired and that's where his anger came from. I just wish I could've been home. He could've taken it out on me instead, but I wasn't home, and now it's my fault that Alaina is here and-"

Paige cut in this time. "*Your* fault? Are you kidding? None of this is your fault. It's not your fault that your dad is the way he is. It's not your fault that you have cancer. It's not your fault that you couldn't step in and be the hero for your little sister. I admire that that's who you are and that you want to protect the ones you love, but don't blame any of this on yourself. Please."

"Thanks, Paige." It would be relieving if I truly believed the words she said were true, but there's still this tiny corner of dusted guilt inside my mind's bookcase. I know there's some way I can try to make this better with my Dad. Not everyone can be fixed with one simple touch, but people can change. People change people, and the world needs more people who aren't afraid of that good change.

July 16 2019

"Mom," I could feel my legs shaking from both nervousness and how weak they are. Instead of trying to balance I decided to sit down and take a deep breath. She was staring at me intently, watching my legs quivering. "I wanted to know if maybe I could see dad?"

It felt weird asking my mom's permission to see my dad since after all, she's not exactly my real mother. She looked at me and stiffened, her eyes squinting a little tighter.

"You want him to come here?"

"Yes." *Not really,* my mind spoke back to me. "I just wanted to see if maybe he and I could have a real conversation." I know he's probably not even interested in coming to see me but it would be nice to have this guilt erased and hopefully make a change in his life.

"Alright," my mom shrugged and checked her watch. It was around lunch time which led me to believe he'd be sober right now but since he's an unemployed man, I could be wrong. It was nerve-wracking to know that my dad could be coming here to talk to me. I can't even recount the last time this happened.

What I Didn't See Before

In a way, I'm lucky that Paige and I both have experiences with bad relationships with our fathers, not really being able to let go of any of the past pain they put us through. Watching her forgive her dad carved a small hole in my heart. God put it there to be patched up, but only I have the right to heal it.

A part of me wanted to wait to do this another day, possibly a day when I'm feeling better or when I know that I won't accidentally vomit on him from the chemo while trying to have a real conversation. Everyday I've been waiting for a moment of relief from the pain, but it hasn't come yet. It feels as if things keep spiraling downwards physically, and things are escalating higher emotionally. The mixture is unsettling, I always used to put my physical feeling before my emotional feeling, but this feels better.

"He can come in an hour," my mom said, her eyebrows were knit together in a tight line. She said this as if she were asking a question, with a bit of confusion, a bit of worry, and a lot of panic. They do get along, her and my dad. When he's sober he's the best guy in the world to her. Everything changes when he's not. The entity that was once in me takes over his psyche and controls him, turning off the switches of positivity. Alcohol can negate the true character of a human being. My dad just so happens to be a victim, and cold turkey isn't the option.

"How do you think he would feel about us trying to get him help?" I asked.

"To be honest, honey, I'm thinking we have to. It's time we start fresh." She smiled at me and squeezed my arm. "I'm so proud of you."

There was never a time my mom uttered those words to me. Nobody has ever been proud to have me in their life. I've always felt like a burden to the world and to the people who supposedly love me. It's been in my head all of this time. My family just wants to see the best me live my life out, not the one trapped inside a cage watching a substance make decisions for me. And now, it's here. My opportunity to make an ashamed son proud of his dad. It's my mindset that's needed to change all of this time. Nobody is too far gone to be loved, and especially to be loved by God.

"He's supposed to be here in like, five minutes." I nervously tugged at my clothes, looking down as Paige watched me.

What I Didn't See Before

"Luca, you're qualified to do this. God gives wisdom when you need it, just ask for it. You're going to be great, okay?"

I let go of my clothes and smiled at her. "Okay."

She gave me a quick kiss on the cheek and left the room. It would be easier if she were here with me in my corner, watching this unfold and giving me advice under her breath of what to say next. But I know it can't be her who fixes my broken past.

Three minutes passed before the sound of a knock on the door startled me. I pulled myself together, taking in one last deep breath before announcing, "Come in."

He opened the door, red flannel shirt, greasy brown hair, eyes stinging red. He looked unwell, but a different unwell. Something has changed.

"Hey," I waved half-heartedly.

He took a minute to answer, wiping the thin tears from his face.

"Why should you talk to me?"

His voice was raspy and deep. It felt like a lifetime ago since we were face to face like this. No punches being thrown, no anger behind our voices, no feeling like I'm

What I Didn't See Before

walking on eggshells. It was difficult, but in a different way.

It's difficult to face someone who is a part of you and tell them what you really think about them and how you feel about their parenting. We're told to honor our father and mother, but to what extent? Where does that line exist that needs to be cut off? I guess it's different for every child. It could be cut off at one punch, maybe two, or maybe the words hurt enough to cut it off then. But for me, it's been years of this excessive torture and I'm just now getting to confront him. One thing I hope for in my future is that I can teach the next generation not to do what I did. This abstinence of not telling him led to: me drinking as well, me getting cancer, my mom's panic disorder to worsen, Alaina to be in the hospital, a broken family, the loss of my dad's job, and a long overdue conversation that feels "too little too late". Maybe it's not. After all, the opposing side of that is "better late than never". It's all about perspective- our eyes need fixing, and there's only one solution on where to focus our attention. Now, my dad and I, son and father, were face to face discussing the respect and honor I should have for him that is now lost. Those words in themselves, I could tell, did a number on him. *Lost.* Aren't we all? Aren't we all just doing our best everyday trying to find the silver lining we so badly strive for? Anything to tide us over, anything to reassure us that our life isn't a lost hope.

That's exactly how it's become for my father. A losing game that's impossible to win. The substances were a way to ease the pain of reality when all it ended up doing was making it worse- and he bluntly admitted to that. There was shame and regret in his voice but there was also a spark of ambition, turning over into a new chapter of life.

Our discussion became more like a sorry-fest of rambled apologies in no particular order. First it was him, mentioning everything he should have done better and everything he did wrong in his life, that he should've been a better father and that nothing he can do will take back what he did. Then it was me, offering my condolences for never having a conversation with him, never telling him I loved him, never wanting to spend time with him, never even acknowledging him as my own father. Of course this happened after I told him how I felt about him without trying to feel too guilty, but still trying to have that honor and respect we should have for our parents. He tried to cut me off a multitude of times, telling me I don't owe him any

What I Didn't See Before

apologies, but I eventually was able to get through how I felt.

It didn't feel perfect after it was over, but it felt like a really good start. We didn't have this awesome divine appointment where God intervened and I started spewing out the perfect words of what I needed to say, but God has definitely given me wisdom every time I prayed for it. The way I was able to speak to him was much different than I would have in the past. I felt smarter, less intimidated, and I was able to articulate my sentences in a way that impressed him- which made me feel pretty good about myself- and he told me he saw a drastic change. I told him about God and how He saved me, but he didn't say much in return about his beliefs. Not everything is going to happen with the push of a button, but God was definitely doing some major work during our conversation. The more I can tell him about Jesus, the more hopes I have of him turning over, which ultimately means that there will have to be some quality time spent with him, which we both badly deserve.

What I Didn't See Before

Chapter 22
Paige
July 15 2019

It was supposed to be a good evening, a quick catch up, then a bite to eat, and maybe a walk in the courtyard. What it had come down to was something none of us expected. Coming here to Saint Andrews has always been my safety net. Somewhere I could go to confide in my best friends, a place where a lot of horrible things happened but also where healing took place. Nothing could have gone worse.

About an hour before heading up, I got a text from Luca that his Dad had dropped by and they were finally able to talk. Nothing made me happier than to think they could patch things up the way my dad and I were able to.

What I Didn't See Before

Luca is less stubborn than I am, less headstrong and less independent, but also less clumsy which allows him to get the job done. He had built up a way with words. My gift is not as strong.

Past tense. Everything about him is past tense. It was quick, or so I heard. The moment I arrived all of my friends swarmed me, not even saying hello but just reassuring me for reasons I couldn't explain. *He just stopped breathing*, they said. *He was asleep, he didn't suffer,* they said. *The doctors did all they could,* they said. But when it's all said and done, when it's too late, it's too late- and I didn't even get a chance to say goodbye.

His dad had his head buried in his chest, sobbing until Luca's shirt was drenched. His warm face left warm marks on Luca's cold dead cheeks, bringing some life back into him one last time. The blue and pale subtle tint of his skin came faster than I thought. I held onto the hope that I'd hear his heart monitor start up again like mine did, and that this would all be over, but I feared that it was much too late now. This very place I am in right now should have been me. I should be the one lying on my deathbed, with the pale blue skin, the tear soaked shirt, and the unwavering body as no breaths came to rise and sink my chest back into

What I Didn't See Before

the earth. It took everything for me not to scream, to throw things across the room until nothing whole was left.

I couldn't sit in the room with his family. I had to get out and go somewhere away from this room. So I ran. I ran past everyone I knew without saying hello, I ran until my legs felt numb, and I ran until my breath was almost out.

Then I stopped. I was in the Chapel, alone, surrounded by nobody but artistic figures, drawings of prophets, stained glass windows, and an altar straight ahead of me. As I walked towards the altar I felt the wind from the ceiling fan blowing gently against my skin, calming my nerves and bringing my senses back to life. I spotted something behind the altar being blown by the fan, making "whoosh" sounds. I drew nearer to the altar and saw what the movement was. A Bible had been left open and the breeze from the fan was turning the pages. I watched because for some reason it was the only thing that calmed me in the moment. All of the sudden it stopped. My eyes fixed on what I needed to hear:

For since we believe that Jesus died and rose again, even so, through Jesus, God will bring with him those who have fallen asleep.

What I Didn't See Before

- 1 Thessalonians 4:14

  There is no reason why I can't grieve. Losing someone is one of the hardest obstacles of life, especially someone you had a deep amount of love and care for. It's not going to be something we can shake off within a matter of minutes, hours, days, or even years, but there's a better place for those who fall asleep. Jesus is celebrating with him. I can just picture Luca dancing to music we've never heard before, singing with a fake microphone of his own kind, feeling no pain and no suffering. A part of me longs to be there too, but my time will come. I have so much life ahead of me and it is not to be taken for granted. Life is truly a gift, whether you believe it is or not, the treasures are hidden in plain sight.

August 2 2019

  I introduced myself to Luca's family a few days later at the funeral with Brett, which was the perfect amount of time for me to pull myself together. The tears have died down massively, but I still cry about every hour, which may be saying a lot about my usage of the word "massively". It's better than before, which in my eyes is

What I Didn't See Before

still a huge amount of improvement. Their Dad didn't seem to know about me which really wasn't a surprise, the mom didn't know much either except she had met me once or twice, but their siblings seemed to know exactly who I was. It made me smile to think about how I must have been important enough for his siblings to know about me. Alaina knew, of course, but I had no idea Devin or Lila knew anything at all.

    We went out a couple weeks later for lunch, my family and his, and got to know each other a little better. There were changes in Luca's dad's behavior. He was more talkative, not as intense as before, and more lively, and even though he didn't have a job, he talked of an opening at this small local hardware company. He seemed enthusiastic about it, and so did Samantha, Luca's bonus mom. He never liked using the term step-mom, so we decided to change it to his bonus mom instead. We talked about my college plans and what my future would look like. I've never worried about making bank and being the richest, instead I've always wanted to do something that makes me feel complete. I still have yet to find out, but I feel like my heart is pulling me to do something with kids. An art-teacher at a Christian school for elementary students has been on my mind, and my family and his really seemed into the idea as well. They said it fits me, and I'd have to agree.

During that dinner, Samantha said something that will always stick with me. It felt as if Luca had implanted those words into her head, and force-fed them to her until they finally came spilling out. There was no other explanation to describe the reason for this was. Joey and I talked about it for days, trying to discover where the sentence sparked from, but we couldn't quite figure it out.

What she had said was, "Even though the whole world mourns, heaven is rejoicing because sometimes a person can only be saved by death."

Luca's dad's eyebrows raised and Samantha apologized for the intenseness of that sentence, but I smiled, because I knew that Luca was home.

Acknowledgments

First off, I'd like to thank whoever made it here to the end of this book and took the time to read what I had to say. It was a long journey for me, but I could not be happier with myself for committing to writing this, even though all of the difficult moments in the past couple of years.

Secondly, I'd like to thank the staff at the Mayo Clinic Pediatric Rehabilitation Program. Without the help of each and every one of you, I would not be living this good of a life.

Thirdly, I'd like to thank my friends Emma and Joe for being such great role models in our journey of healing together. Both of you have a very special place in my heart and I cannot thank you enough for all you've done for me.

Lastly, I would like to thank both of my parents for supporting me. I've been able to discover my purpose in life because both of you have allowed me to experiment with different plans all the while still supporting me, even if my plan was ridiculous. I love you both and cannot thank you enough for all you do for me.

About the Author

Alexandra Davidson is an aspiring author from Medina, Ohio. She currently attends Cleveland State University majoring in Creative Writing. After several years of dealing with medical issues, Alexandra was finally diagnosed with POTS (Postural Orthostatic Tachycardia Syndrome), and has been tackling multiple other chronic illnesses as well. In managing her health and having to do high school courses online, she began writing as a method of coping and soon found how passionate she was about writing. Her first novel, *What I Didn't See Before*, published at the young age of 18 is loosely based on her experiences at the Pediatric Pain Rehabilitation Center at the Mayo Clinic in Minnesota. Alexandra is also strong in her faith and feels that Christ should be the central focus in her work.

Made in the USA
Coppell, TX
16 March 2021